SUNDAY BEST

a novel by

Bernice Rubens

SUMMIT BOOKS
NEW YORK

Manufactured in the United States of America
1 2 3 4 5 6 7 8 9 10

Library of Congress Cataloging in Publication Data

Rubens, Bernice.
Sunday best.

I.   Title.
PZ4.R8913Su   1980   [PR6068.U2]   823'.914
79-27131

ISBN 0-671-40081-9

For Sharon and Rebecca

Part One

1

Just because I'm writing a book doesn't make me a writer. Let's get that straight from the start. My only problem is that if I ever finish this book, it might give me ideas. I might want to write another, and yet another. So just in case I'm going to be a writer, I must guard against writing my first book in the first person. I could say it all happened to 'him'. That would at least envisage his present, his future. But with the 'I', there is only past. 'I' is final; 'I' is the recognition of death. 'I' is not for the first book, but the last.

You see, you write a paragraph and already you think you're a writer. Already you're worried whether this might be your last book. Maybe, when all this is down, I will have said it all, and there'll be nothing more to write about anyway. Not that that ever stopped a writer. But with God's help, when this is finished, I can shut up and start living a little. No more books, and I can afford the 'I'.

So I take in my hand that thorny pronoun. Forgive me my histrionics; writers are prone to dramatize themselves a little. It's a lonely job, and there's little drama in the making of it. So allow me my thorns, let me grasp them, let them bleed me a little. My pleasure. Let me drop them when they get too painful, and you'll have to make do with the 'he' for a while. Let George Verrey Smith feel them in his rotten flesh. It's easier for me that way.

But since this is the beginning of my story, you must know where I stand. So I pick it up, that nettled pronoun, and hold it gingerly. I am going to touch it with myself, and plunge straightway, for I am a devout coward, into the shallow end. My name. I have no problems with that one at all. Neither with my address, though the latter is subject to change. It's the other headings that fox me. Age, *curriculum vitae,* referees. Such proclamations wither me, and might even reduce me to the 'he' again. But bear with me, if you are still there, that is. I am moving into an honest, self-revealing phase, so that, although I already feel myself a writer, I don't kid myself about my compulsive qualities, and I humbly address myself to those who are still with me, to regard this preamble as a final rehearsal for the gentle movement of my tool of thorns towards my body. It is here. I am ready to name myself, and savour it well, for not only is it a name to conjure with, but it is the one solid thing about me of which I am absolutely certain. My age, my profession, my testimonials, in these I have no confidence or conviction whatsoever. But my name, challenge it at your peril.

George Verrey Smith. It doesn't look that good on paper, but I promise you, that rolled off the tongue by the Major Domo at the dinner of the Society of Authors – I'm not an ambitious man; my sights are painfully low – take my word, such as it is, that that name has a noble ring, that much more will be heard of it, even if you care not to listen. George Verrey Smith. It will stand repetition, even in writing. Notice the lack of hyphen. The hyphen is a legal appendage, an indication of a name in law. But my name is blood, pure blood, and marriage had nothing to do with it. Get that straight, 'cos I don't want you to start thinking that my wife has contributed anything to my being, well or otherwise.

I'm going to get my age over quickly, because I like to pretend I'm not sure of it. Even so, I hesitate, since hesitation about one's age gives one's readers a loophole. So give or take a year or two, it's, er, forty-two. I am now faced by what I take as a personal affront; *curriculum vitae.* I have never heard that phrase spoken. It is a phrase of cowards, and only written down, and I intend to ignore it. For all the jobs and activities I've taken part in during my life I find utterly irrelevant, and so for your sake and mine, I shall spare you all that. And generously will offer you a re-cap. My name is George Verrey Smith, I am – er – forty-two years old, my profession, that of a schoolmaster, and I no longer have any confidence in my teeth.

10

There. I've said it. And it was supposed to be the last thing I would tell you and I've blurted it out like a solution without a problem. So we'll have to go back a little. I'll start at the beginning, which is not, after all, a surprising place at which to start. I had a nanny once, who, off or on duty, looked like a fashion model. One afternoon, she went for a walk and was run down by a taxi. They took her to hospital and undressed her. The poor woman confessed that never in her life had she had a bath, and changed her underwear only when it fell off her. Her immaculate topping marked her as a fraud. Now there was a woman who didn't begin at the beginning. I won't be referring to her again, so I might as well tell you that as they peeled off her grey chemise she expired. Whether from shame or injuries sustained, I cannot tell, for there was no post-mortem. In any case, how can you tell if someone has died from dirty underwear? My wife, after all, is hale and hearty. I'm not saying that a bath and clean underwear would have saved my nanny from the taxi, but at least, had she known to start at the beginning of things, she might have died with a less unsavoury reputation. So mindful of my poor old nanny, God rest her soul, I'm starting with the start, whatever that means, and I'm going to tell you the root of all my troubles, whatever that means also. I mean, even if you're talking about yourself, and perhaps, as by now may well be the case, *to* yourself, you must have some respect for chronology. Otherwise, there is nothing but confusion. So roots are beginnings, and my teeth are the root of my problem. Now you may think that this is a small matter, but when you're pushing – er – forty, and you're already afraid to look too closely at your hair, when snow is not as white as you remembered it, well, this is no time to begin losing confidence in your teeth.

It started about a year ago when I picked up an apple. I am, or rather, was, a great apple-eater, but there was something about this one apple, this year-ago apple, that suddenly assumed a look on its mottled face of such scorn and mockery, that I knew better than to argue with it. During my life, I have taken up most challenges that have been offered me. I have always had, as it were, a fighting chance. I'm not a man to shirk a challenge. But I'm wise enough to know when I'm beaten. I put the apple down, and fingered my front teeth, my long-standing apple teeth. They wriggled with gratitude at my decision. Since that day I have never touched an apple. I have nurtured in myself such a loathing for apples. They were a signal to my present condition. In fact, I might as well face it. The root of my troubles is not teeth at all. It's apples. You see how roots can shift, and beginnings meander. Maybe my nanny, God rest her soul, was not so very wrong after all.

So to hell with chronology. Neither forwards nor backwards shall I go, but rather, like a crab, sideways, for in such direction is less chance of collision, and what with my nodding teeth, this can be a decisive factor.

So off on a tangent to my breakfast this morning. She'd just put the tray before me, she, being my wife, whose name, even in thought, I find difficult to refer to. But for what it is worth, I give it to you, for after all, she did you no harm, so why should her name stick in your throat. Joy. Believe it or not, that's how her mother named her. Imagine. I have noticed that it is a name that has a habit of appending itself to the most joyless of creatures and my wife is no exception. Well, I sat there this morning facing my toast, porridge and fried sausages. She has a habit of bringing everything at once, and keeping me waiting for my coffee. It's her own special brand of efficiency, tho' I know it by no other name than spite. The sight of the toast unnerved me. As I spread it with butter, I deliberated which part of my mouth could safely accommodate it. The sole back molar on the left side was normally my only toast tooth, but even that, over the last few days, had painfully rejected calls on its function. That too, like the others, was loosening. I considered giving it a rest, thinking that in idleness it might tighten itself. Desperation can often blunt a man's intelligence. I could of course, have dipped the toast in my coffee, if she ever got round to bringing it. But I withdrew from such an abdication and started with confidence on my porridge, confining the mixture to my four wriggling front teeth, good for little else now save pap. I decided to give a miss to the toast and to test my right molar on the sausages. Damn

12

her with that coffee. Her place had been discreetly cleared away except for a few crumbs that surrounded the white damask ring where her plate had been. The crumbs irritated me, yet another reminder of her lack of thoroughness. Everything about her, apart from her underwear, was just that much short of perfection, but it's this small deficiency that unnerves me so much. She might as well be an out-and-out slut. She tidies my study, for instance, till not a speck of dust remains, but she constantly neglects to place my pens in line, and their lack of symmetry infuriates me. She leaves the cushions unplumped; the drawers of my tallboy are never one hundred per cent closed, the counterpane is always uneven on one side. And now those crumbs she'd left around her plate. For a moment, I considered hoisting my body from my seat and removing them myself, but such an act would be a surrender, a participation in what, after all, is her duty to me. And I am a firm believer in not giving an inch when a mile is takeable. So I weighed up the intensity of my own irritation on the one hand, and the effort and surrender of clearing the crumbs myself, and the crumbs and my irritation won the day. Where the hell was she with that coffee? I loathe her heartily.

Now you may think from all that, that I do not love my wife. But I don't hate her either. Tho' it's difficult. The point is I've treated her rather badly over the past few years, and that's enough to make you hate anybody. She's been so decent about it all, and it's this full-blooded decency of hers that fills me with loathing. Yet I can't hate her. I've never been able to leave her either. If two such negatives add up to anything at all, well, that's more or less what I feel for my wife.

I checked on my teeth again. Panic-loose. I must go to a dentist. Perhaps now, in any case, it's all too late. You'd think I'd have something better to do than to sit here testing my teeth. You'd think a man like myself would have real problems. You're right. I have. I'm trying to concentrate on my tooth problem, I tease those left-over molars of mine with sausage meat and pap, because the real problem, I cannot face. I play safe with a touchable, tangible problem. I have to. I daren't allow my mind to stray to anything else. Because, many years ago, but the guilt is as sure as yesterday, I killed a man.

There. I've said it. Or rather, I've written it down. To say it aloud invites an echo, a magnification, and it is enough, what I have done, without enlargement. I dare not risk it aloud. I write it down. I minimize my sin with pen and ink, or rather with the stub of a pencil, which is close, close to the page, with the proximity of absolute confession. So I whisper with my crayon, 'Long ago, I killed a man.' *Il y a longtemps, j'ai tué un homme* – a hangover from my translation days, before I started to make my living at the blackboard. I often translate a predicament if it's too tough to handle. I reduce it to a job of work. *Oui. J'ai tué un homme.* But it was no Frenchman's doing. It was my very own.

Does it show on my face? Lately I've found myself avoiding mirrors. Was this a rehearsal for an act that I would never indulge in again? And is it for this reason that I cannot look my wife in the eye for fear of what I would find there? My wife is very clever and her understanding has been my undoing. Other men complain that their wives don't understand them. I complain because mine does. She has always insisted on understanding me. She has destroyed me with her understanding. But I have destroyed too, and I must get back to it and take upon myself the blame. I must leave my wife out of this, tho' this too, damn her, she will understand. I married her when I was twenty-one. It was not my first mistake. I had made many before, but minor ones that I could have rectified, had they been important enough. But my marriage was a major error. Not marriage itself. I have nothing against marriage, but at twenty-one, for a man, it is foolhardy. Moreover I was a virgin. I didn't know I was. In fact I thought I wasn't. That might give you some idea of how much of a virgin I was. I am not sure to this day whether my wife was or wasn't, and later on, when I learned the facts of it all, I had already forgotten the circumstances. It is a great omission in one's life if one does not know whether or not one has married a virgin. I have always been too embarrassed to ask my wife out of fear

14

of betraying my own ignorance. In any case she would laugh at me and remind me of it. She exploits my secrets at every opportunity, not in playful private teasing, but in public malice. But I must not speak ill of her. I have done her great wrong. She is a victim, and therefore unaccusable.

I want to start at the beginning, because I need to know myself how it all started. I have problems with what is relevant. I remember sneaking into a church when I was a boy and spitting into the baptismal font. I had walked about half a mile through the town and over the tombs in the churchyard, gathering saliva all the while. I gathered it with relish and deliberate intent, tho' what my purpose was, I had no idea. Then I saw the font, and the cause of my harvesting became clear. I dropped it neat and clean on to the holy slab, and I watched it trickle down the side, holding its integral shape all the while. I don't know why I am reminded of this incident at this time. Did that act of blasphemy have anything to do with that man who lies rotting in the earth? Everything is relevant, and nothing. I am digressing again. But in truth I am postponing. I will start at some sort of beginning and promise to go straight to the end. But this is a vain promise from a man whose whole life has followed detour after detour. But as a token of my honest intent, I shall leave my shadow on the straight and narrow, as hostage as it were, as I digress into my meanderings. And after my detours, I shall ask myself, 'Where was I? Where was I?' and pick up my shadow again to lead me to the point of my story. I will try. I will start at the beginning. Not with the teeth. When you look for the root of your problem, you're really looking for someone or something to blame. No one is to blame except myself. This I have learned. My scribblings have not hoodwinked me. Forget the teeth and the apples. This is really the beginning of my story. My stubby pencil trembles on the thin straight line, and my ill-fitting shadow ploughs the way.

2

We have neighbours, my wife and I. The Johnsons. You will notice in my story, that apart from my own name, which makes you feel at once that you are in the company of a better class of person, all other names are very banal, common even. Which makes you feel that the story could have happened to anybody, not you, of course, but at least to your next-door neighbour. And in fact, this story did happen to the Johnsons as well as it happened to me. So think again. It could happen to you also.

The Johnsons had been married for fifteen years, and had kept their charlady all their married life. That's the sort of people the Johnsons were. Everything always went right for them. Mr Johnson did-it-yourself, Mrs had a slender wardrobe, but always the right thing to wear for the occasion. I've seen inside her cupboards, but I could have told you without looking that she had trees in her shoes. Everything about the Johnsons was in its right place. They did no one either harm or good. They were totally unaccusable. The Johnsons were what is known as a *nice* couple and everybody loathed them.

I had a nodding acquaintance with both of them, which is unavoidable, I suppose, if you're neighbours. I would see them on my way home from school, always together, in a desperate armlock which I found unnerving. They were both very tall. Laid end to end, they would have covered lengthwise their twelve by nine Axminster on the living-room floor, or their lounge, as they chose to call it. Though they were not the sort of people you would associate with lounging. One wondered indeed in what position these two giants slept, tho' sleeping, like lounging, was an activity difficult to associate with them. For they were always up and doing, cleaning their car, weeding their front lawn, even sweeping the small square of pavement that led from their gate to the kerb. For me and for all the others in our street, their activities on a Sunday morning were a fair eyesore, and a row of net curtains were hastily dropped at the sight of the Johnsons's infuriating energy. I would watch them from my study window on a summer Sunday, see them settle in their car with Tom their son and a picnic basket, and there was no doubt in my mind that wherever they were going, along with thousands of others who were going to the same place, Mr Johnson would find somewhere to park.

As I dropped my net curtain those summer afternoons I often offered up a fervent prayer, that one of these fine days, one of the Johnsons would come a cropper. And God is occasionally good.

It happened on a Sunday that I remember very well. It was apple Sunday, and had marked the first apple that I had had to deny myself. I'd gone up to my study, tickling my teeth on the stairs, and in such a profound depression that I went straightway to the window to refuel my melancholy with the sight of the wretched Johnsons at work. But their frontage was deserted. Their car stood at the door, gathering whatever dust was available, and a few sweet wrappers shamed the garden out front, shedding a sudden humanity on to the whole house. And then I heard Mrs Johnson screaming. It was a cue for all the net curtains in the road. Within a few seconds we were rewarded with yet another scream, and then another. Things were hotting up. In my excitement, I even forgot my tooth problem. The silence between the screams was as promising as the screams themselves, but Mrs Johnson herself put an end to the show by crying out, 'Help, help. Please stop him.'

The row of net curtains dropped like frosted eyelids on business that was not their own. Now I don't know what made me different from the others. I am a monumental coward, and what made me rush downstairs and into the street and up the Johnsons's drive, I shall never know, and had I stopped to think I should have turned back. I had time to retreat as I stood at their door banging on the knocker. My knees quivered and I badly wanted to relieve myself. But I banged away, having no thought of what I would do once inside. The screaming continued as the door gently opened, and young Tom, terrified, stood blinking in the gap. I squeezed myself in. The screams were fainter now, and I feared that I had arrived just in time for the kill. But first things first. 'Can I use your bathroom, Tommy?'

He boggled at me. Had I come just for that. Didn't I have one in my own house? Or was he just astonished that a schoolmaster, and his form-teacher at that, was subject to natural functions like anybody else. I'd never been inside the house before, but I ferreted out that bathroom with a kind of survival instinct, and bolted the door. For some reason I felt safe inside, and the strangled whimpering from below stairs did not bother me. I took my time with my toilet, staring at my parts with a loathed compulsion. I hated this position, that I, like all men had to assume at least three or four times a day, and the enforced necessity of viewing oneself. A woman, if she so wished, could live out the whole of her life without confronting her gender. For a man it is impossible. And at each confrontation, I was filled with disgust. Perhaps had I been able to put my parts to better use than the mere tool of natural function, I would have felt less hostile towards them. I ought to tell you at this juncture in case it isn't already very obvious, that my sex-life is practically non-existent, and has been such for many years. I could tell you all about it, but it would be a digression, or perhaps I use that as an excuse, for it would also be very painful. But whatever the reason for my withholding the truth, I intend to proceed with my story. It would be a relief indeed to take my mind off my present toilet position, with any digression whatsoever, but not that one. Any reflec-. tions on my inadequate sex-life would stun me into dumbness. Once you've started on your confession you've got to get on with it, but I've no intention of exposing myself to unnecessary pain by confessing with each and every part of me. For that I could go to an analyst, and because I was paying, would have to tell all, or else not get my money's worth. But this confession is free, and I am entitled to be generous with it or other-

18

wise. I don't know why it should bother me that there are certain things I don't want to tell you about. I am not, after all, in any way beholden to you. But I will not be nagged into total confession. I can and will be silent when it suits me. I will not be bludgeoned into complete exposure by anybody.

I've got to get off this subject. I am trembling with an indignation that seems to have no source. It is doing me no good, this confession, and I must get back to that Johnson bathroom, or lose my sanity.

Our own bathroom is a complete reflection of the state of our marriage, and I have a fancy that all couples reveal, or rather betray, themselves in their bathroom furnishings. Ours, for example, is clinical, with a permanent smell of disinfectant. It has, it is true, a lingering lavender odour, but I am not for one moment fooled by that one. There is nothing in our bathroom that isn't white, unless it's hidden away in the white medicine cupboard. Even our soap is white, always. And there is a double lock on our door. It is a room for ablutions and toilet only, and nothing beyond these two functions could conceivably take place within. We have a white clock too, which is my own contribution. I don't know what my wife does in there, but she takes an inordinate time doing it, and sometimes, if I have the opportunity, I set the alarm before she goes inside. She has never referred to the clock, although she's probably been jolted off her seat more than once by the bell. I suppose she understands, like she understands everything, tho' I don't know the meaning of it myself.

Now the Johnson bathroom was a different story. It was completely unorganized, and yet it looked neat and clean. I suppose it was the colour; a duck-egg blue, which softened corners and reflected whatever dust there was with its own colour, thus making it acceptable. And even if it was just plain dirt, I found it far less disgusting than I would have had I found it in my own house. Often one can leave one's neuroses behind, and more often than not, they are left in one's bathroom, since there, they come most spendidly into flower.

There was a bookcase filled with paperbacks, and this piece of furnishing attracted me too, though the titles were ones that

I had spent many years dissuading my pupils from considering. Clearly, there was more to be done in this bathroom than
the mere washing of hands. In my position, I was directly
facing the window, and the shelf which held the Johnson dis-
guises. Divided into two sections by a giant china soap con-
tainer, her cover-ups were on the left, and his on the right. But
in the middle, directly in front of the soap-container, stood a
tin of denture cleaning-powder, and it irritated me that there
was no clue as to which side of the partnership it belonged,
and I resolved at my next meeting with the Johnsons, which
threatened to take place pretty soon, if I was to justify my
presence in the house, at that meeting, I would investigate
whose choppers were portable, his or hers, or possibly, since
the powder was in the middle, theirs. I wiggled my teeth again.
At least I still had them, and I assured myself that as long as I
laid off apples, I would keep them for ever.

I buttoned my fly, and wondered what to do next, and as I
stood marvelling at their neatly folded bath towels, it occurred
to me to run myself a bath. I still wore my dressing-gown, and
had missed my bath that morning. The apple incident had left
me too depressed. But now, for some reason, I was feeling
infinitely better, with the determination and courage to visit
the dentist the following day. It seemed to me to be quite
natural to take a bath while still undressed, and I ran the hot
water at full speed to drown the moans that persisted from
below. I lay in the bath, completely submerged, avoiding confrontation, and sailing a rubber duck across my chest. We have
a rubber duck in our bathroom, a white one of course, and
apart from the clock, my sole contribution. My wife, some ten
years ago, had actually had thoughts of giving me a child, and
I remember the excitement with which I had bought that duck
as my first preparation for its arrival. Since then she has made
many promises, but I know better than to invest in rubber
ducks. I know, and she never ceases to remind me, that her
own mother died when she was born. She is afraid, she says.
But she's lying. It has nothing to do with that. She simply
doesn't want to lose her figure. Now I know that if I'm writing
in the first person, you are seeing my characters only from my

point of view. But believe me, in the case of my wife, there is no other viewpoint. Anyone else would tell you the same. I am not trying to prejudice you. These are the facts I am giving you, and one can prejudice only with opinions. Another fact is that she offered to adopt a child. I am giving her her due. But I could never see the point in that. You'd never know where it came from, and after all, it wasn't as if I couldn't manage one myself. She actually stopped sleeping with me too. She wasn't going to run any risks, she said. So I went and found it else-where for a while. And of course, she understood, and there is nothing more calculated to put an end to an extra-marital affair than one's wife's understanding.

I shoved the duck away, and the ripple revealed my parts again. I got out hurriedly and dried myself with the 'her' towel. I wondered for a moment what had brought me to the Johnson bathroom, and then I realized the full impact of my whereabouts. I put my ear to the door, but after a few minutes it was clear that the performance below was over. The silence unnerved me, because it made less plausible my presence in their house, leave alone naked on the bathroom mat. (Hers.) I dressed hurriedly, tho' now, whatever had happened was over, and beyond anybody's interference. I wondered whether I could slip out of the front door and back home without being observed. As long as young Tom was not waiting in the hall-way. I decided to make a bold dash for it, and almost tripped on my dressing-gown as I ran down the stairs. I reached the front door, where Tommy, from nowhere, blocked my way. He was very white and I heard him trembling.

'Go an' look,' he said with an accusing hostility that was quite beyond me. 'Go an' look wot she done.'

'Go and look what she did.' I corrected. I felt the need to delay, and I was playing for time.

'Go on,' he insisted. 'Go an' look.' He was not prepared to correct himself and prove my victory, but neither did he want another rebuff, which the young lad would have got most cer-tainly, for I am, first and last, a schoolmaster. 'What has she done?' I parried.

'Go an' look. You'll see,' he said.

'Surely it's none of my business,' I tried.

He sneered at me. 'You 'ad a bath in our 'ouse, didn't you?'

I refrained from aspirating him. He was right. Having used their bathroom, I was practically one of the family.

'I'll go and look if you insist,' I said nonchalantly, trying to imply that it was only a joke he was playing. I dawdled towards the living-room door but Tommy didn't follow me. I would have given anything not to go inside, and heartily wished myself back in my own study, behind my net curtains and like everybody else in the street, minding my own business. Tommy was staring at me while I waited, with such a look of hatred, that I felt that whatever lay behind that door was my responsibility. As indeed it was, as I was soon to discover.

I raised my hand to knock on the door.

'You don't 'ave to knock,' he said with assurance, as if there were no formality inside that requested privacy. 'Go on in. See wot she done,' he risked it again.

But I knocked on the door again, and waited. There was no answer. And now, glad of an excuse, I turned to go away. But Tommy was quickly at my side, in command of the situation. He kicked the door open, and practically pushed me inside, while I resolved to punish him brutally in class the following day. But I quickly lost all thought of Tommy as I was confronted by what lay on the living-room floor. Mr Johnson, the whole length of him, his curly head neatly filling the great angle of the hypotenuse on their triangled red Axminster. And there was no doubt about it that he was dead.

'Who done it?' I stammered, infected by Tommy's outrageous lack of grammar. I looked up and saw her, sitting dumbly, her hair ruffled, her blouse and skirt torn, gripping one furry bedroom slipper in her hand. She struck me at that moment as being quite beautiful, and I quickly looked back at her late spouse again, as I suddenly recollected that tin of powder on the bathroom shelf. His mouth hung open, and thank God, his dislodged dentures claimed ownership, and I sighed with relief that the powder would never be used again. I had thoughts of bending down to his mouth and refitting them, to add perhaps, a little dignity to his passing, but sod him, I thought. He'd probably deserved whatever had come to him, and I was too moved by his wife to feel any sympathy in his direction. Then I noticed that his eyes were open, and I realized that this was the first corpse I had ever seen. I do not know by what instinct I knew that Mr Johnson was dead. There was no blood on him, nor sight of any weapon that could have reduced him to that position. But I knew that he was dead, and probably looking as my father must have looked when his ticker gave out. I had flatly refused to look at my father's body. Corpses should be avoided wherever possible, and I gave little thanks to Mr Johnson that I had accidentally come upon his. He reminded me so much of my father, tho' they looked not one whit alike, that I wanted to pick up one end of the carpet and roll it over him. I was in no mood to be reminded of my father, I can tell you, and I see no reason why I should tell you why. My father was a bastard, let's leave it at that, and I have no intention of giving him even the thinnest of immortality with my feeble pencil. Let him rot and let's all forget him. He was a drunk and he brought no good to anybody in his life and to some people a great deal of harm. I know you're thinking that this is no way to talk about a father especially if he is dead. You can think what you like. It's my father and I can do what I like with him. No wonder Mr Johnson reminded me of him. They both had it coming to them.

I swung round on Mrs Johnson, and for some reason I shouted at her. I felt like a policeman. 'What happened?' I said.

She began to cry. Now in normal circumstances, a woman's tears will drive me from the house, I spent most of my childhood running away from my mother, though you can think what you like, I won't go into that one either. I cannot bear tears. They are the worst form of blackmail, and I will not be cowed by them. But for some reason, with Mrs Johnson I stayed put, probably because I feared that my exit in any case was blocked by her horrible son. I went over to her, and bending down, caught sight of her breasts through the rip in her blouse. They heaved as she wept, and I hoped she'd weep for ever. I waited, allowing a silence, which I thought was only decent in the circumstances, while gulping an eyeful of cleavage. I timed that silence rather well, I thought, then, covering her hand with mine, I repeated the question softly.

I felt like the hero of an exceedingly 'B' movie.

She did not look at me, but neither did she move her hand. 'He just collapsed,' she said. 'He had a bad heart, I know.'

'But you were screaming. He was hitting you.' I wanted him to have earned his death.

'We had a quarrel,' she said.

I felt it pointless now to ask what the quarrel had been about, but she was already pouring it out between the sobs, and tho' her voice was highly charged, there was something flat about the whole narration, a bland unaccusing recital of facts. He had accused her of having other men. It was no new accusation. He was insanely jealous, and any seemingly irrelevant annoyance would spark off the charge. Over the years, she'd put up with it in silence, denying it time and time again, as indeed, as she claimed, she had every right to. But suddenly, she had had enough. Yes, she offered that there had been other men, plenty of them, and then, to give him his money's worth, she told him that even Tommy wasn't his. It was at this point that he'd started hitting her, and demanding the name of Tommy's father. She hated him by now, and smarting under his blows, felt absolutely no need to withdraw her story. So she had just said the first name that had come into her head.

She trembled at this point in her story, and so did I, and for good reason. For whose name is on the tip of all tongues? What other, than George Verrey Smith. He stopped hitting her to ask for a repeat, with which she obliged. Now if any name is to be reckoned with on a second take, it is mine, and he promptly collapsed and she supposed it was from his heart.

My immediate impulse was to go over to him and tell him it wasn't true. I had, on all accounts to clear my name. I knew it was useless, but I did it all the same, and when I'd put him in the picture, I turned and did the same for her. 'You know it's not true,' I said. 'Why me, of all people?'

24

She started crying again. 'I suppose it's because you're a neighbour. You just came into my mind.'

I felt a tinge of insult that this, in her mind, had been my sole qualification for putative fatherhood.

'I think Tommy heard it too,' she added, throwing off this last piece of information as if it were of no importance.

I rushed outside to see if Tommy, eavesdropping as I had no doubt, had heard at least the truth of the story. But he was nowhere to be seen. I came back into the room. 'Look,' I said patiently, 'it's terribly important to know whether Tommy heard. Did he, or didn't he hear?'

'I don't know,' she said helplessly.

For a moment I lost sympathy with her, realizing my own predicament. 'We have to find out,' I said, but I realized that she was in no state to deal with this problem, and that she needed some practical and immediate help. I phoned her doctor, mother and sister, and rallied the forces that she feebly volunteered. I made her some tea, and forced her to take a little brandy. I was suddenly anxious to leave, and I patted her forehead as a preliminary gesture of leavetaking. I gave her promises to return, and to send my wife to console her, and I covered as well as I could my haste to get out of the door. And there outside, from nowhere, was Tommy. I looked at him for some clue, and there was the same hostility in his eye. I decided to take the bull by the horns.

'I'm not your father, Tommy,' I said. 'Your mother was very overwrought.'

He let me pass in front of him and I felt his eyes on me all the time. He waited for me to open the front door. Then he shouted, 'You are my father. My mother told my Dad, and I hate you.'

I hated him too at that moment, but resolved to postpone thinking about him, until I could do so calmly. My main purpose at that moment was to get back to my own house, rush upstairs to my study, bolt the door and collect my thoughts. I looked forward to tickling my teeth for a while. Moreover I had not yet looked at the Sunday crossword. And I toyed with the idea of putting on my Sunday clothes. And what with thoughts of my neighbour's demise, I had a full morning in store. Life was good.

But it was not to be. The hall was crowded with women and a sprinkling of their husbands from the neighbouring houses. I had been seen entering the scene of the crime, for crime it had to be, and they had gathered to await my return.

'What happened?' my wife shouted, as soon as I got a foot in the door. She was always speaking on everyone else's behalf. She was a born chairman.

'I'd rather not comment,' I said, mindful of the desperate telly interview. 'No comment at all,' I added with authority, and with the hint that there was a great deal to comment about. Mrs Pratt from the corner double-fronted, stared at me with hatred. She had spent the waiting period salivating in anticipation, and now her mouth fell open and the spittle dribbled down her hostile chin. She would never forgive me. I pushed my way through the unfriendly crowd and managed to get half-way up the stairs, when a shrill voice called my name. 'Mr Verrey Smith,' it rang out, and I enjoyed hearing it. It is a name, you must admit, that needs to rend the air if it is to be savoured in its full splendour. I let its echo subside before I turned. The call came from Mrs Bakewell. I knew it was she, because the calling of a name like mine cannot but fail to leave an aura about the person who has voiced it. Besides which, her mouth was still open, Mrs Bakewell being slightly adenoidal.

'Mrs Bakewell?' I queried. I had never liked her. Her language was irritatingly prim. Every syllable was dry-cleaned before uttered. And she was much taller than her husband, which was what I hated her for the most, because I had no doubt, in fact I knew, for I had known them both before their marriage, that at the time of their wedding they were both the same size. Over fifteen or so years, she had pecked away at him with her tight mouth, and laundered vocabulary. She probably gave it to him only for Christmas, or on his birthday. I didn't even get it on those days, which probably accounted for my mounting hostility to the woman, and at this reminder of my long abstinence, I could have killed her. 'You wanted something?' I sneered.

'You were in the house,' she said, hanging each word out to dry, 'while a lady was screaming. Perhaps you were involved,' she threatened.

My hatred suddenly inspired me. 'That was no woman screaming, Mrs Bakewell. The screaming came from Mr Johnson.'

'Rubbish,' she spat, 'that was a woman's voice.'

'So it sounded,' I said with dignity, 'but it came from Mr Johnson after his wife had cut off his balls.'

That'll teach you, I thought, you frigid bitch, and the red flush that rose up her cockerel neck and blanched about the gills rewarded me, and proved that it had been well worth the try. I left it in the air and turned to go up the stairs. I felt that down below, no one, not even my wife, knew whether or not to take me seriously.

I locked the door of my study. I had much to think about. After all, it was not every Sunday that I became a father. But why me, and it was this thought, out of all the morning's activity, that lingered and most excited me. It was surely no accident that she had given my name. I know, and so do you by now – I have laboured it enough – that it is a good name, but there are dozens of men in the street whom she knows by name. And yet it had been mine. I had thought of my hyphenless handle in conjunction with many a profession; an explorer, a club secretary, a surgeon even. But an adulterer, never. And I began to have thoughts.

I do not relish such thoughts, and there is only one way, for me at least, to get rid of them. If I put on my Sunday clothes, my lustful thoughts evaporate. It is an infallible cure for adulterous fancies, and though, as I grow older, I get the disease less and less frequently, I seem, for some unknown reason, to become more and more addicted to the cure. So I went to my wardrobe for my sundays.

I keep them in a separate hanging compartment, because they have nothing to do with the man who wears my ordinary clothes. I opened the cupboard and viewed my range. It is very limited. I have never actually gone so far as to pay out good money for my sundays. I make do with what my wife gives me. I've told you before that she is very understanding. She is tolerant and even indulgent of this little hobby of mine. She has given me her pink chiffon, her blue taffeta and her indispensable little black, that turned out to be not so indispensable after all. I am a little short on trappings and trimmings, and my only jewels are a string of her imitation pearls. Sometimes, I would slip into her bedroom and borrow some ear-rings, but I was not prepared to face that crowd in the hall. I debated which sunday to put on, and I decided on the chiffon, remembering that I was down to my last pair of nylons, and that the chiffon was long enough to hide the ladders. I laid out the dress, the underwear, the shoes and stockings on my couch, and I started on my face.

My vanity case was my last birthday present from my wife. She bought it especially for me, and its contents are extremely generous. First I applied my moisture cream, which is a must for a base, and in my make-up, as with most things, I am very particular. I waited a while, while my skin absorbed the cream. If you're to make a good job of maquillage you have to be patient, and since this is the most exciting part of my Sunday ritual, I am prepared to spend a long time at it. I love the pan-stick application that comes next and the sudden transformation it affects to the texture and colour of the skin. A little rouge, high on the cheek bone, to give contour to the bone structure, then a mere soupçon of lipstick to offset what would otherwise be an interesting yet sickly pallor. My eyes came last, and to these I gave my all. Eye-shadow, eye-liner, lashes and mascara. And when it was all done, I added my blonde wig. This last I had originally bought as a birthday present to my wife, but I could not bring myself to part with it, and bought her a fountain-pen instead. To this day she does not know of its existence and I feel slightly guilty every time I put it on, though I console myself with the thought that it probably looks much better on me.

I took my time with my dressing, and had a little difficulty in closing the back zip – one of the hang-ups of dressing alone – and when it was done, I looked in the mirror and found it pleasing. I sat down in my chair with my legs neatly crossed at the ankle, and picked up the crossword puzzle. Between clues, I fingered my chiffon or patted my hair. All thoughts of Mrs Johnson had ceased, and I was at peace with myself.

I ask very little from life. My tastes are very simple, and in such moments of happiness, I can even think of my wife by name.

3

I would get on with my story if I could, but I keep thinking of
my father, and such thoughts are an obstacle to any undertak-
ing. But I must not think of him. It is imperative to put him
out of my mind. I can remember him only with hatred and
bitterness, a bitterness that corrodes. I am not ready to think
about him. When I can recall him with a modicum of affection, that will be the time for nostalgia. But I don't ever want
to think of him with affection. Yet I can't not think about him.
I am trapped in his leprous growth across my mind, an im-
mortal cancer on my brain. I will not speak of him.

There was a post-mortem, of course. I am speaking of Mr
Johnson. My father had one too. It was an accident, they said
about my father. But there are accidents and accidents, and
even my father, as he lay dying, knew that it was no accident.
But enough of that. Mr Johnson's post-mortem showed unsur-
prisingly that he had died of heart-failure. So everybody was in
the clear, and the neighbours tried to hide their disappointment. But all that came much later, and I must go back to save
what little chronology I have forged for myself.

I went to school on the following day, taking a roundabout
way to avoid passing the Johnson front door. I would be
spared Tommy for at least the week before the funeral, a week
to put my thoughts in order, and to organize a plan of action,
if indeed, there were to be one at all. I had a vague hope that
Tommy would never put in an appearance again, indeed, that
both of them would move out of the neighbourhood, or with
luck, out of the country altogether. People said Australia was a
good place, a happy hunting-ground for those who had failed
elsewhere. The advertisements called it the start of a new life,
and it struck me that Mrs Johnson and her wretched son,

could do worse than to forge a new path thousands of miles away from George Verrey Smith. I resolved that at our next meeting, I would tentatively suggest that a change would do her good. But I kept thinking of those weeping breasts of hers, and at such thoughts, I didn't want her to go.

I had difficulty in settling down to my school work that morning. Monday, in any case, was a particularly heavy day on my timetable, and to make matters worse, Mr Parsons, our junior French teacher was away with what he had spluttered through the telephone was 'flu, but knowing Mr Parsons, was probably his Monday hangover. And so I was saddled with his work as well as my own, and far worse, with Mr Parsons's form, who frightened the life out of me. They were in what we call the Remove, a name in my opinion which should have been acted on forthwith, for they were a bunch of zombies who neither gave nor took took any trouble. They constitute the embryonic 'Don't knows' of a gallup-poll society and the 'Yes, definitelys' of the vox pox telly interview. Their indifference to play and learning was sublime, and I found their cluster of blank staring faces, unnerving. I settled them down to an essay on 'My favourite holiday', a classic time-filler and waster, and rushed off to my own form, where the noise and chaos were almost refreshing. Tommy's desk stood empty in the front row, and its proximity was menacing. I toyed with the idea of displacing him during his absence, but I knew there would be no volunteers for a front desk. It seemed the ambition of most of the boys to spend their schooldays as far from the centre of learning as possible, and on the first day of every term there was a veritable stampede for the back row. It was only the meek, but not necessarily the inheritors of the earth, who ended up in front. And Tommy, with half a dozen others, had been brutally sieved through the seven rows in the class-room, and had landed, bruised and complaining in his present, though absent, exposed position almost touching the black-board. Had I been my own pupil in that position, I would have been terrified. So, on second thoughts, I decided that Tommy should on no account be displaced.

I teach in a Comprehensive school, and we have a fair cross-section of pupils. I have often heard parents praise the school for this very reason. By 'cross-section', the middle-class parent squares his conscience with the jolly knowledge that his little Roger is in the same class as their charlady's boy. And the charlady, touched too by the cross-section syndrome, delights that her Albert is mixing with a nicer class of person. But when *I* say cross-section, I have no axe to grind, and I mean quite simply that the pupils are poor and rich, together with a slight quota of 'coloured', who for some reason never seem to qualify for an economic category. They are simply 'coloured', and that, I suppose, says plenty. Our headmaster, a man of the cloth – I shall go into him later, preferably with a knife – our headmaster, the Reverend Richard Baines, is very proud of his coloured quota, limited as it is. They are his token guests, a handful in each class, whose black presence silences any suggestion that the Reverend Richard Baines is faintly prejudiced. He is a firm public believer in voluntary repatriation, but privately, they should all go back where they came from, tho' a good number of them were born a stone's throw from the school. Often, at the end of assembly, he can be seen sweeping through the centre aisle – from the balcony, I get a top-shot eyeful of his black gown and mortarboard – patting the odd crimped head to display his large humanity. His coloured quota, I may add, is strictly limited to the lower forms. He is dubious, he once confided to me, about the older negro boy. 'They develop so early,' he said, coughing discreetly behind his hand, a gesture that left no doubt as to what category of development he meant. But I digress again, and I do not relish it, for the headmaster reminds me of my father, both bullies, but my father less so, perhaps. At least, he was always drunk, which offered some explanation for his behaviour. But the Reverend Richard Baines is a bully, sober. But I don't intend to discuss the merits of either. There is little to choose between them, and let them both rot.

I got my class to some semblance of order, and started out with the register. I ticked off the answers as they came, and didn't even bother to call Tommy's name half-way down the list. But a register, especially towards the end of the school year, and it was already spring, has been subconsciously learned by rote as efficiently and as meaninglessly as the Lord's Prayer. Try saying, 'The Lord is my shepherd, He restoreth my soul', and await the price of your omission. 'You missed out Tommy Johnson,' came a roar from the back row. The omission of Tommy's name had thrown out the known rhythm of the register as if a foot had been dropped from a term-long persistent iambic pentameter. 'What about Tommy Johnson?' they persisted.

'He's patently absent,' I said, pointing to his untenanted desk.

'So's Terry Burley,' they shouted, 'and you called *his* name.'

'I happened to know in advance that Tommy Johnson would not be in school today.' Why the hell was I defending myself, I thought. I had made a mistake, that's all. But I had already made an issue of an otherwise completely insignificant name.

'What's the matter with him then?' The back row again. There never seems to be an identifiable voice from the back row, but wherever it comes from, it speaks for them all.

'Unfortunately,' I said, 'his father died.' It was one way of getting silence, and I toyed with the idea of using it again in some other context in an emergency. They stared at each other and then at the inkwells on their desks. Whatever people may say to the contrary, it is still possible that a class of twelve-year-old secondary modern boys can occasionally be moved to silence. It went on for a long time, and I felt they were unconsciously celebrating the late Mr Johnson with a two-minute shut-up, and I doubted that he deserved such a memorial. 'I knew 'im,' one of them said at last, seeking a closer proximity with a man who had temporarily achieved a celebrity status.

'So did I,' said another, with contempt. 'So did lots of us. You weren't the only one. 'E was orlright, old Mr Johnson. 'E used to 'ave that clean car.'

' 'E wasn't so old, was'e?' said another. 'When's the funeral, Sir?'

'Yes, when, when? So's we can send flowers.'

They were wallowing in it now, and their chatter dispersed

into little groups, excited, lump-in-throat chatter, of an event that had broken the monotony of a Monday morning.

'Poor old Tommy,' one voice was heard amongst the din, and they fell silent again, as they came to relate the pain with one they knew, and possibly with the awareness that their own fathers too, were mortal. I took advantage of this silence to call them back to concentration, and I finished off the register. I had decided to be very kind to them. I had one week in which to establish myself as a kind, God-fearing, pure and modest schoolmaster, who wanted nothing but people's good. A concrete image, indestructible, and impervious to the accusations and tall stories that Tommy no doubt would scatter on his return. I am not a man who goes round fucking other people's wives, was what I wanted to say, and I had a week to make it clear. I looked at the rows of faces, and lost heart. It was a moment in which I had a tinge of doubt that I was not the boy's father.

But mindful of my resolution to present myself as unimpeachable, I sought ways and means of making such an impression. You see, I am not by nature a kind man, and it is always an effort for me to display a generous disposition. Moreover a Monday morning was not a propitious time to put such a resolution to the test, for it was the day devoted to an assessment of the week's work in all subjects, for which I, as their form-master, was ultimately responsible. Normally I would go round their desks examining each set of exercise books in turn. It was usually a morning of terror and silence, a routine that called invariably for reprimand and punishment. A fine time to have sudden notions of charity. Yet I had only a week, and there was no time to be lost. So I decided on calling the boys up singly to my desk. Kindness in private, especially when out of character, is less embarrassing than kindness in a mass. Each pupil would think himself solely favoured, and would hold my generosity as something of a secret, in which only he and I shared. I would imbue the whole class with a sense of private and single privilege, so that when the crunch came, as come it must, an army of protest and disbelief would rise naturally to my defence.

I called on Jack Tindall, the mainstay of the back row, deciding to start on the worst and to get it over with. He was surprised to be chosen as pioneer of the new procedure, and he gathered up his books, such as he could find, and in his bewilderment, stumbled over the outstretched legs punctuating his way to the front. Normally the back-row boys anticipated these hurdles, and a boy's passage from the back of the class to the blackboard was normally in the form of a slow canter, but Tindall was so bewildered by my sudden calling, that he forgot the fixed fences on the way. He landed on his face below the blackboard. Time for kindness and concern, I thought, and was grateful for a natural opportunity. 'Are you all right, Tindall?' I said, surprised at the gentleness in my voice, and fearful of how true it was ringing. The prostrate Tindall was more thrown by my concern than by his minor injuries, and it took him some time to rouse himself from the floor. His books, loose-leafed, and shoddy already, were sadly depleted by his fall, and it took a little time to collect the dirty scraps of paper which Tindall passed off as his homework. My concern had unnerved him, and already before spreading the scraps on my desk, he was apologizing for his lack of diligence, for his neglect of his work, for his thorough no-goodness, and promised to do better the following week, and for ever and ever, Sir, and to pull himself together. The class were stupefied by Tindall's submission.

Amongst them, there must have been a slight feeling of letdown, and thoughts of who was the bully-elect, now that Tindall had joined the Establishment. Tindall was practically genuflecting by now, and feeding my natural inclinations to cruelty, but I kept my kind head, alarmed at the thought that goodwill was possibly another name for blackmail. I dealt with Tindall as quickly as possible, tho' the sudden silence of the whole class made privacy difficult. I gave them my permission to chat quietly amongst themselves until their turn came, but their misgivings at my generosity silenced them.

It was difficult to find anything good to say about Tindall's work, such as he had done, but with his promise of a better start, and a new leaf, I dismissed him quickly because I knew that if he humbled himself much longer, they would lynch him in the playground at break, and I already had one murder on my hands of which I was not guilty.

I took each boy in turn, and stunned them with my concern, and they returned to their desks, paralysed by my goodwill. Each felt himself the favourite, and though outwardly they maintained their bombast, fearing to lose caste as the teacher's pet, inwardly, or so I liked to think, they had sworn eternal allegiance to the cause, right or wrong, of George Verrey Smith. It was a good beginning.

The bell went to signify the end of the lesson, and there was actually an audible sigh of regret across the classroom. It was the first time in my career as a schoolmaster that I had heard such a sound, and I could not help but relish it. But I must take a hold on myself. I don't want to get too soft.

I went back to the common-room for a quick cup of tea. There was a crowd and murmur about the notice-board, and when I managed to worm my way to the front, I understood what all the noise had been about. A large printed notice in red capitals, announced the calling of an extraordinary staff meeting at the end of the day, and grudging apologies for the necessary overtime. Now the Reverend Richard Baines was not a man given to hyperbole or histrionics. He was the understatement, not, as he thought, out of subtlety, but out of the conspicuous lack of anything of interest to say. So that when our clothed boss called a meeting extraordinary, then extraordinary it must be, and over our tea, there was much conjecture amongst the staff as to its matter. Miss Price, the Scripture teacher, and our only woman member, who had been on the staff longer than any of us, and was close to the Reverend's ear, kept a pointed silence and a fixed look of disapproval about her chin. Whatever the extraordinary meeting was about, it was no doubt serious, and there was also no doubt that Miss Price was in the know. Mr Gardiner our man in Geography, offered the suggestion that Baines wanted yet again to limit our coloured quota, and if so, he, Mr Gardiner, would certainly have a word or two to say, but Miss Price's unchanging inscrutable look did not favour the possibilities of that offer. Mr Lewis, panting from P.T., suggested that it was something to do with the gymnasium, and the mishandling of equipment by the extra-mural classes after hours. Mr Lewis firmly believed that nothing that took place outside the gymnasium or playing fields, could possibly have anything to do with education, but a quick glance at Miss Price's face confirmed that his suggestion was way off the mark. We kept our eyes on her face while we threw out possibilities, reduction in salaries, longer lunch duty, shorter holidays, and it was only when Mr White from Chemistry, bored with the game, and with complete frivolity, tossed off the suggestion of immoral practices amongst the staff, that Miss Price's eyelids were seen to flicker, and a clue was at hand. But whether they had wavered on account of her own personal modesty, or because there was a glimmer of truth in Mr White's proposition, was hard to assess. I myself felt suddenly unwell, and so overwhelmed by my own feelings of guilt, that I quickly convinced myself that the staff meeting extraordinary was on my account, and I turned to my locker to hide my trembling from the others. I had thoughts of going straight to the headmaster's study and confessing. But to what? To the suggested fatherhood, or to my Sunday hobby? How could he know about either, unless Tommy had already sneaked into school, hot from the corpse, and spilt the beans. I found myself wondering which exposure I would prefer, since the one confirmed my manhood, while the other radically questioned it. Some choice. I would deny both, of course, the one with justification, but what possible evidence was there of my innocence. Tommy's word against mine. I had no children of my own; that was a known and staff-room-pitied fact. My wife was to blame, they had no doubt murmured, so it was natural that I should sire elsewhere.

Tommy's story would be wholly believable. But 'I didn't, I didn't', I heard myself saying, 'I didn't m'lud, that's not my scene. I've got a wardrobe of Sunday clothes to prove it.' I shuddered at the sensation such evidence would generate, and I truly couldn't decide within myself which guilt was preferable. I returned to the tea-drinking crowd, and threw out suggestions with the rest of them. My isolation and non-participation could have singled me out, and I shuddered at my sudden intuition of all manner of self-defence, as if indeed I were a criminal. 'Perhaps it's just the Reverend creating a little bit of drama, and all it's about is who is going to open the school fête.' I tried not to look at Miss Price, but out of the corner of my eye I saw her sneer, and I knew that it was not a sneer at the suggestion itself, but at the quarter from which it came. I knew now with irrefutable conviction, that I was in the dock, and I shivered.

I don't know how I got through that day. I plodded through my classes with my kindness, but it was a kindness that was killing me. At the end of the day, I rushed blindly into the headmaster's study. I was the first to present myself, and I composed myself on a chair with as much dignity as I could muster. I felt like an aristocrat of the French Revolution, who, not wanting to cause a delay, stood waiting for the arrival of the tumbril.

4

They arrived in groups, or singly, with Mr Hood, the music-maker, absentmindedly whistling in the rear. The Reverend glowered at him, but Mr Hood, a man after my own heart, stared right through him, and not only finished whistling his air, but added a coda for good measure. The Reverend Richard Baines, to whom a perfect and imperfect cadence sounded exactly the same, and on whom the finesse of a coda was completely lost, felt his authority questioned.

'That's enough, Hood,' he thundered.

'It's finished,' Hood said with satisfaction, and he smiled with an innocence that I envied.

Miss Price took her seat beside the Cloth, with a smug 'I'm-in-the-know' look smeared on her face. Mr White placed himself in front of me, and I was glad because I could steady my foot on the back of his chair to stop my leg from trembling. During the course of the day, I had half-heartedly composed a speech in my defence, half-heartedly, not because I was unaware of the urgency of my case, but because I was unsure of the charge. So I was obliged to fashion a defence that would answer to the charge of Adultery and Eonism, no mean assignment, I can tell you. I had in the end decided on a flat denial of both, and if my wardrobe were called into question, it was the overflow of my wife's, and as for Tommy's story, he was a bloody liar, and what his motive was I couldn't imagine. In fact, my whole speech was one of righteous indignation at their suspicions. How dare they cast such aspersions on a God-fearing upright citizen like myself. By the time the Reverend Richard Baines was ready to open the meeting, I had worked myself up into such a state of hostility, that I had to fumble at nothings in my brief-case to hide my rage. Mr Gardiner, sitting next to me, remarked on my sudden sweating and hoped I didn't have a cold coming. I coughed to oblige him, and hoped the same for myself, while the Reverend waited until my feeble wheezing had subsided.

'Ladies and Gentlemen,' he began. He always pluralized Miss Price, tho' she had hardly enough about her to indicate even one of her kind; flat-chested and overall hirsute, it was difficult to determine her gender except perhaps by touch, if anyone could bring himself to do it. She tut-tutted at her chief's incorrigible sense of humour and waited agog for him to launch the tidings she had already juicedly savoured.

'I would like to apologize to Miss Price beforehand,' the Cloth continued, 'for having to discuss what you will agree is an unsavoury subject in her presence.' I hung on to my chair, and I felt my bowels melting. All memory of my speech had evaporated, and I felt myself swaying.

'But I thought it best,' he went on, 'to confide in her the matter of this meeting, so that she would be well prepared to withstand whatever embarrassment would ensue. I apologize to her once again.'

Miss Price smiled. 'I hope I am broad-minded enough,' she said, 'to overcome the delicacy of the situation. But a trespass is a trespass, and must be dealt with.'

A nodded approval from the Cloth. 'Let us pray,' I expected him to say, and I myself at that juncture felt in need of a prayer, a good solid, infallible invocation that the Reverend and Miss Price would lose no time in dropping dead. I inadvertently lifted my leg from Mr White's seat and set up such a vibration throughout the row that Mr Gardiner was convinced that my cold had burgeoned into pneumonia. This time there was less sympathy, and he shifted his seat to avoid contact. I wanted very much to cry.

The headmaster smiled at Miss Price, and I wished to God they'd get their wretched bonhomie over and done with. He coughed and composed his face with a seriousness that indicated he was coming straight to the point. 'You will have noticed,' he said, 'that Mr Parsons is absent from school. You especially, Mr Verrey Smith,' he offered with a sick smile, 'would have noticed his absence, since the bulk of his work has fallen and will continue to fall on your shoulders.'

His use of the future tense heartened me a little, and I returned a smile that was a mere arrangement of my features, rather than an expression of goodwill.

'You will have been told that Mr Parsons has the 'flu,' the Reverend went on, 'but I am bound to tell you that Mr Parsons, in body at least, is perfectly well, but that I have found it necessary to suspend him from his duties until an inquiry is complete.' He left a pause for anyone imprudent enough to ask why, but we all knew better than to question his authority. The answer would surely be forthcoming. As for myself, I trembled less, tho' I still did not feel absolutely in the clear.

'I have called this extraordinary meeting,' he went on, 'because it has come to my notice that Mr Parsons has been indulging in perverse practices on the school premises.'

My body slackened, and I slumped in my chair, overcome by a mounting fit of giggling that I could not control. The relief that I felt at my acquittal was finding its full expression. And while rocking to and fro with my convulsions, I desperately sought some excuse that would account for my hysteria. Mr Gardiner eyed me with horror. Whatever the cause of my outburst, it was certainly no symptom of pneumonia. Most of the staff shifted with their disgust, and a few of the more generous amongst them thought I was simply mad, and I wondered whether I should offer to the Cloth a plea of temporary insanity. By now, I was laughing aloud. Bless you, Mr Parsons, I said to myself, you poor little bugger, but bless you and your buggery for putting me in the clear.

'I fail to see what is so funny, Mr Verrey Smith. Perhaps you would care to explain yourself. This is a very serious matter.'

I took him up on it, feebly inspired. 'It is because it is a serious, and, I may add, a tragic matter, that I laugh, in the same way that I laugh when told of someone's death. My laughter is close to tears, Headmaster.' It was a game try, and I think it convinced nobody. But then nobody could call me a liar, and I was by then able to control my hysterical relief and to assume a serious air. The headmaster decided to be satisfied, and to drop the subject since he had no notion of how to handle it.

'If I could have your attention,' he went on, 'I would like to tell you how the matter came to my notice, to outline the events, so that you will all have a true picture. A situation like this one is open to all kinds of rumour, and I want you to shut your ears to it, and to remember only the facts that I shall give you. The decision as to what to do with Mr Parsons is mine and mine alone, but as his colleagues, you are entitled to be aware of the facts that make any decision on my part necessary.'

That, in a nutshell, was our headmaster's version of democracy. He often referred to his 'game little band' of staff, and dropped us tit-bits of confidential matter, professing an interest in our opinion, but determined to ignore it. He had already made his decision. Of that there was no doubt. Mr Parsons would get the push, and the Reverend, who was a vindictive man, would make jolly sure that poor old Parsons wouldn't get another job. It struck me that Parsons was a very unfortunate name to be saddled with such an offence and I wondered whether our chief was taking it as a personal affront to his own collar. Poor old Parsons. Apart from my own personal indebtedness to him, I felt wholly on his side, and I was determined that, whatever the consequences, I would fight to get him a square deal.

'The Parsons affair was brought to my notice by a parent of one of the children in the lower forms.' The headmaster had already put Parsons in the dock. He had robbed him of his title and reduced him to a case. 'The parents shall be nameless,' the headmaster went on, 'but I feel it pertinent to the case to tell you that the child concerned is one of our coloured quota.'

I wondered how this fact in any way shed new light on the matter, or new dark, as the case may be.

'I intend to make an issue of the case simply because the child concerned is coloured, and I want it to be known that the cudgels will be taken up on behalf of any pupil, irrespective of his race or creed.'

'I fail to see, Headmaster, that the colour of the child concerned is in any way relevant, and why a larger issue should be made of the case simply because of this factor.' I was pushing my luck, I knew, but an innocent man, or rather, an acquitted man gains strength and courage to defend others, and at that moment I would have devoted my entire life to the cause of Parsons's acquittal.

The Reverend Richard Baines was not pleased. 'You and I, Mr Verrey Smith,' he said with loaded tolerance, 'do not see eye to eye on some matters. I have no intention of arguing the point. To me, the colour of the child is a decisive factor. There is no point in pretending that we are all the same and that society draws no distinction. I make an issue of the colour of the child in order to underline the justice of my system.'

I was happy for the Cloth that he had at last found his pet little nigger. I sneered as audibly as my position would allow, as much at Baines as at the other members of the staff who seemed to find nothing unsavoury in his very own brand of discrimination.

'If you would allow me to continue, Mr Verrey Smith. I hope you understand of course that I am under no obligation whatsoever to divulge this story to my staff, but I believe that this is a school problem and should be understood by all those in authority.'

If he thought he was putting me in my place, he was mistaken. I was prepared to hold my tongue only as long as he had his say.

'The child's mother complained that over the past few weeks the boy has been very sullen and given to fits of rage. It appears that a few days ago the child, at the end of his tether, confided his problem to his mother. It would seem that Mr Parsons had a daily assignment with the boy after school hours behind the maintenance shed in the playground. I leave it to your imagination what the nature of that assignment was.' Then, after a pause, doubtful that we had imagination enough, or perhaps because he himself relished the telling, he added, 'In fact, the child was brutally assaulted. With or without his consent is an irrelevancy.'

A unanimous gasp from the staff from all except myself and Mr Hood, who whistled instead. In the extreme circumstances, the Reverend was willing to overlook his music master's eccentricities.

'I am very concerned with the matter,' the headmaster went on, 'because there may be other boys involved, coloured or otherwise, Mr Verrey Smith.'

I held my tongue. What else could I do? If you defend a pervert vociferously enough, the backlash could be on you. You could well be accused of obliquely defending yourself. I was beginning to lose appetite for the Parsons campaign, and I disliked myself a little for my cowardice. The headmaster was at it again. 'I want you all to be on the look-out in your classes for any unaccountable sullenness, to investigate it as delicately as possible and to bring all your findings to me. Boys are secretive about this sort of thing. They are ashamed and fear recriminations. But often a sensitive boy will break down under the strain, and I want you all to keep your eyes and ears open. Any seemingly insignificant piece of information is important. I have every intention of getting to the bottom of this matter.'

He was blissfully unaware of the aptness of his metaphor. I allowed myself a little giggle. I was entitled to that after all, and felt no need to excuse myself for it. He was closing the meeting and thanking us for our attendance, as if we had any other choice, and as he rose, he called, 'Mr Verrey Smith. A word with you, if I may.'

I trembled. Was it possible I was not completely in the clear, that out of deference to my feelings, he had chosen privacy for my private prosecution. I hung about, fiddling in my brief-case to give the others time to get out. Miss Price, the eternal aide-de-camp, made no show of making herself scarce, and I was obliged to present myself to both of them.

'Mr Verrey Smith,' he started. 'I find your overall behaviour at this meeting hardly creditable.' A nod from Miss Price put her squarely in my opposition. 'Your laughter, which, I take your word for it, was possibly hysterical, is one thing. But your questioning of my sense of justice is quite another. I shall handle the Parsons affair in my own way, and let me be absolutely honest with you, Mr Verrey Smith. Perhaps I am doing you a favour in telling you this. It casts no savoury reflection on your own character if you are bent on defending a man like Parsons and his practices.' Again I found his phrasing apt, and I smiled a little.

'I am sorry if you find this a trivial offence, and one wonders what, if anything in your eyes, would appear criminal. When, in the year 1927, in the case of Brown versus Jones Jnr the learned barrister Charles L. Johns defended Brown in the case of sodomy, there was a body of opinion that felt that in his vociferous protest Johns was defending himself. Remember that, Verrey Smith,' he roared at me. 'A man is known by the company he defends.' He opened the door for me on this last remark, and gave me no opportunity for reply, even if I had been able to think of one. And as I walked down the corridor back to the staff-room, my confidence waned considerably. I didn't believe his story. The Reverend Richard Baines was not the kind of man to have such information at his fingertips. I was convinced that he had made up the story as he went along. He had no confidence in his own argument, and had perforce to avail himself of evidence from better minds than his own, invented or otherwise. Even so, this thought made me feel no better. I had a sudden urge to go home and get into my sundays. The Reverend Richard Baines had unnerved me completely. He had made me feel guilty, and again, I did not know of what charge. I decided to by-pass the common-room, not wanting to face the gossip that surely must be simmering, gossip about myself as well as poor Mr Parsons, and I went straightway to the cloakroom to get my coat. As I crossed the playground I made an elaborate detour to avoid the maintenance shed. I felt that the Reverend Richard Baines was spying on me through his window.

5

Over the years, I have inevitably thought of my father whenever I have indulged in Sunday dressing. In the intention, the art itself, and the after-taste, thoughts of my father persist. And though such thoughts are a curse, my appetite for my hobby is overpowering, and I would not dream of forfeiting such pleasure even if it meant that I could discard my father from my mind. I knew as I left the headmaster's study that my only escape route into peace of mind was through my wardrobe, and I hurried home, through the back lanes, avoiding the Johnson door. I tried to think of Parsons and what would happen to him. What was indefensible was not his perversion but his stupidity. At least I had involved no one else in my aberrations, and I had to fight down a strong feeling of self-righteousness. My father would have killed a man like Parsons. He had a pathological aversion to any trait in a man that could possibly be construed as womanish. Even gentleness did not become a man, a theory that all his life he managed to put into practice. I don't want to think about him, but I cannot think of Parsons either, and as I quicken my pace towards my wardrobe, he voids my mind of all but himself; he pounds it as he pounded my chest as a child with a viciousness he hoped his paternity could confound. He tramples on my nerve-ends as he trampled those icy fields, pitch in the winter mornings, dragging me over the hard-frosted grass that pierced my toes with fire. 'Come along then, breathe, breathe, open your lungs, man', and he would pound my chest to bruise it open to the menacing fresh air. I don't want to talk about him. It is too late now anyway. I am er – forty-two, and my teeth are panic-loose, and a man lies rotting in the earth. If now I were to tell you about my father, or even to tell *me* about my father, would my teeth tighten and that man resurrect? Would I have to cast off my wardrobe too in order to come to terms with him or must he remain the eternal discordant accompaniment of my only joy?

A crude man, my father, a bitter man, a drunk with a loosened vulgar tongue. I hear his voice, his voice in my mother's bedroom at the end of a drunken orgy. 'Clap yer thighs shut, woman. Yer meat stinks.' With a father like that, who needs literature. I hate him, I hate him, because in the end he forgave me. One day, I will have to tell you about him.

I am weary of this confession, and find myself eager to get on with my story which would excuse me from further exposure. But I know it to be cheating. The real story is that which went before, the story that engendered this thin narrative line that I am trying to get away with. I remember how often in my childhood I wished him dead, and sometimes now I wish he had survived so that I could wish him dead again. But he cut off that hope for me by actually dying, and now I can only wish him to rot, a poor plea, for he will do that in any case, and without my participation. He is beyond my evil eye. I was more comfortable, I suppose, when he was alive.

He would drag me over the fields – our home was isolated – our nearest neighbour, two miles away. Every morning, tho' in the winter I thought it was still night, I had to shadow his demoniac stride across the fields, and all I had to look forward to was the cold shower on my return. 'I'll make a man of you,' he shouted, and I thought for many years he was talking to himself. Until the first time he forced me under the cold shower, running back and forth from the garden with handfuls of snow to rub on my body. And when I shivered, he hit me, and said I was like a woman. It was then that I started to hate him.

But I have spoken of him enough, and I feel no better for the telling. I know what I ought to tell you about my father, but that is the one thing I shall never tell you, at least not yet, so early on in my story, for it could prejudice you, and I have to be fair to myself. Perhaps when I am dying, I shall whisper it out, for it is a secret that would not lie easily in the grave.

But should I shed it now, much else would peel off with it, including, heaven forfend, my Sunday clothes. So I'd sooner settle for the disease for the cure is too costly. Let him rot, my father. I shall try not to speak of him again.

I was glad that my wife was out when I returned home. Although my study is absolutely private and it is on pain of death that she enters, I always feel more free when my wife is not at home. Her presence, no matter how muted, is an invasion, an onslaught on my train of thought. So I took my time with the dressing, talking to myself all the while, a practice I can indulge in only in private and when I feel free. What I say follows a repeated pattern, and it is a practice for perfection in women's speech and mannerism, rather than the matter of her words. For women, as we know, are not given to intelligence and what they say is of secondary importance to their manner of speech. Or perhaps I should modify that a little. My wife, after all, is highly intelligent, but not intelligent enough to hide it. And there's the rub and why I find it hard to call her by her name. But that's not true. It is not her fault that I cannot name her. I dare not, for it would be an admission of the wrong I have done her.

It was a good dressing day. My make-up was flawless. The Parsons affair and the Reverend's veiled warning seemed trivial, and I blessed my escape route for giving me an inner peace. Other people find that peace in work; I like to think it is none the less valid if found in pleasure. I adjusted my wig, which today sat easily on my head, its fall of ringlets masking the tell-tale shoulder bone. I found myself moving towards the window, and was excited by my boldness. I had been tempted before, but fear had always overcome me. Because what I wanted more than anything else was to display myself and be taken for a woman. I even went so far as to raise the net curtain, and felt such a boundless physical joy inside me that it was almost unbearable. I saw people coming out of the Johnson house, mostly neighbours, and my wife amongst them. I dropped the curtain, and returned to my desk, savouring the after-taste of the joy that had come from self-display. And I knew that there was only one logical conclusion, that I must venture abroad and pass myself off amongst strangers as a woman. It had always been a secret wish of mine ever since I had started Sunday dressing, but until that moment, having availed myself at the window, I had been totally unaware of the delights that would ensue. Now the ambition to go abroad as a woman took a strong hold on me, and I knew that until I had done it, and done it again and again, and succeeded in my disguise, my life would be less than fulfilled. When I think of it now, it was a madness I suppose. I had enough trouble with Tommy Johnson and the Parsons affair, without laying myself open to greater risk, but the need to carry on an open disguise persisted and even the nagging thoughts of my father scarcely blunted the pleasure of my design.

I heard my wife come in through the front door, and a little later up the stairs to my study. 'George,' she called, 'are you ready for some tea?'

I sensed a friendliness in her voice, and dressed as I was, found no difficulty in responding in the same tone. But as my voice left my mouth, I heard its womanly tones and inflexions. 'Yes dear,' it said, 'I shall be down shortly. I must change my clothes.' My voice, which is normally tenor, had reached contralto without strain, identifiable, as I liked to think, with an unmistakably seductive woman. I trembled for her reaction. It was not immediate, and I sensed that she was debating her acceptance or otherwise of my new role. Then after a while, 'Don't bother to change, Georgina,' she said with a giggle. 'We'll have a hen's tea-party. I'll ring Mrs Bakewell to come over.' And I heard her run down the stairs and the ping as she lifted the receiver.

There's no question about it. My wife is sick. My appetite for disguise slackened, and I felt a surging resentment towards my wife. By so readily accepting my little habits, and moreover, inviting the neighbours to share the fun, she had reduced my needs to a game. And what is more, a game I must play with her. I had no desire to appear before Mrs Bakewell and my wife as George Verrey Smith in disguise, as if it were a game of charades. I wanted to hoodwink everybody, strangers, as well as what was left of my own family, that I was indeed a woman, and an attractive woman at that. I took off my clothes, angry that I had to depend on my wife for a wardrobe, and resolved to syphon off from my next pay-packet sufficient to buy myself a complete set of attire of my own choosing. This resolve heartened me a little, as I changed into my school clothes, I tried to concentrate on where and what I should buy, trying to oust the creeping thoughts of my father. I heard the doorbell, and guessed that it was Mrs Bakewell who would lose no time in gathering any possible tit-bit of the Johnson affair. I wondered how she could face me after our last insulting encounter, and I thought of ordering my tea in my study. But I was anxious to discover any developments that had taken place next door, and whether, God help me, there was a whiff of Tommy's story. My curiosity got the better of me, and as my wife saw me coming down the stairs, I could see her disappointment, as if I had let her down in front of her friends. But I had no intention of playing her personal freak, which is what she would have ultimately made me, that was available for display at her pleasure.

'You changed,' she said. 'You didn't have to bother.'

'Thought I'd look decent for Mrs Bakewell,' I said, greeting her as she came in through the hall. She had decided to sulk, and her greeting was coldly polite, and I felt it my duty to jolly up the tea-party. I had let my wife down. I had insulted Mrs Bakewell. It was up to me to make amends.

'What's the news next door, then?' I asked as my wife poured tea. 'Poor Mrs Johnson. It's so young to be widowed.' I tried to strike a balance between a sympathy that might have betrayed me and a callousness that might have seemed feigned in order to protect myself.

'She doesn't cry,' my wife offered. 'Not a tear. I find that hard to understand.'

'I don't think she realizes what's happened to her. It was so sudden,' Mrs Bakewell said meaningfully. 'I mean, no one's too sure how it all happened.'

I felt her eyes on me. I dared not look at her, fearing that she had changed into Miss Price. 'It was a heart-attack,' I said, stirring my tea, tho' I take no sugar. 'That's what Mrs Johnson surmised. You don't suspect anything else?' I said, daring to look at her.

'Well,' she said coolly, 'it'll all be sorted out at the post-mortem.' They both looked up at me quickly to catch my reaction. But a post-mortem on Mr Johnson was one of the few events of which I was not afraid. But I could not help but shiver at the recollection of my father's autopsy, how I sat nervous in the ante-room with my mother, melting with my guilt, tho' I knew that whatever they found in my father's cranium, there would be no traces of trip-wire.

'The funeral will be delayed then,' I said. It was a logical reaction. I could be as bland as Miss Price if called upon. 'Did you see Tommy?' I threw it off as casually as I could.

'He was behaving very strangely, I thought,' my wife said, 'almost as if he wanted to kill everybody there.'

'And no doubt one who wasn't,' I thought. 'Poor lad,' I said. Nobody could suspect my sympathies in that direction. 'I suppose they'll have to sell the house,' I said hopefully.

'It's not hers,' Mrs Bakewell said. 'It belongs to the insurance company he worked for, and I gather she can stay in it at the present low rental. Well, she'd be a fool to move, wouldn't she? Where could she find a house for that money?'

I tried to recall Mrs Johnson's weeping breasts to give myself some joy of her staying. But I still thought of Australia as a better idea, and at a propitious moment, I would put it to her. 'I don't know,' I said airily, 'she's young, attractive, a woman like that should start a new life, go somewhere new, Australia or somewhere, marry again. A boy needs a man's hand.' There was no harm, I thought, in enrolling my wife and Mrs Bakewell in my antipodean campaign.

Neither reacted in the least to my suggestion, and their silence made me regret that I had put it forward.

'There may be reasons that she has to stay here,' said Mrs Bakewell, and I knew that she was looking at me. I had nothing to feel guilty about but I had been accused, albeit by a little boy, and every chance remark was construed as knowledge of my guilt. I knew I had to pull myself out of this incipient paranoia if I was to keep my head until it had all blown over.

But how could it ever resolve itself? What would convince Tommy that I was not his father? If his mother succeeded in persuading him, he would have to face the fact that his mother had lied. And for what purpose? A row, a quarrel. What great dimensions had such a quarrel that it merited such an outsize lie? We could both deny it to the boy, gently and appeasingly, but what evidence would he ever have in his life that our story were true? I was sorry for him. He could not even hate his father as I did. He could not even wish his father dead, because he could never be sure if his father had anticipated him.

I excused myself from the tea-table. I had once again to be alone, not with my sundays, because my father was part of that deal, and I was too disturbed by Tommy's dilemma to confuse myself with my own depression. I reached my study and locked the door. I seriously toyed with the idea of admitting young Tom's paternity, and wondered whether he would grieve less if told of Mr Johnson's deception. I tried to imagine how I would feel if my father were suddenly discovered to be somebody quite other than the one I knew, and whether I would still be plagued with those leprous thoughts that battened on my mind. I realized that whatever Tommy chose to accept, he was in a state of bereavement, and that only time, if he could give time, time, would lessen his grief. I picked up my wig where I had thrown it on to the divan, and twirled it around my finger, and I wished my father alive, so that I could wish him dead again.

6

My father was a butcher. He was born in a butcher's shop of a long-suffering mother, who helped her husband with the mince and easy cuts. My grandfather rushed her to the back of the shop, and finished off the delivery as he might have degutted a chicken. My father smelt of meat from his birth, and died with the smell still upon him. His six weeks' stay in hospital had kept him from sight of a carcass, but he departed to his Maker as high as he had arrived. I suppose a birth amongst offal must tamper somewhat with one's psyche, but I would not hate my father any the less if I understood him. People have been born in worse places than a butcher's shop, and have died mourned by their sons. In any case, the smell of one's father, whether of offal or aftershave, is the smell of neither of those sources, but the simple smell of fatherhood, and all else being equal, I might have loved my father whatever his effluvium.

When I was born, my father was already pushing forty, and was still known as the butcher's boy. I suppose it must have humiliated him, and I must make allowances for that too. When I was four, as my father had been born in that shop, so my grandfather died, full of blood and bread as he cleavered his last chop. My father laid him out in the back room out of sight of the customers and returned to the shop to close what were now his own shutters. I do not remember my grandfather, and so I have no recollection of my father except in the role of boss-man. But I do remember that we moved house and that the move took place shortly after my grandfather died. The move was in fact into his house, large dark quarters sprawling in the middle of a field some miles out of the town. It was too big for us, as it had been too big for him, ill-fashioned for economy. Most of the rooms would one day come in handy, but they never did but to pepper my childhood with cobwebs and ghosts. It would have been a relief to escape to the fields had they not been my father's punishing grounds, and I saw them only as ice-cold confessionals open only on the bleak mornings of winter. I would no more have dreamt of playing there, winter or summer, than I would of shooting dice in the Tabernacle. So my bolt-hole was the attic room, where I slept and had nightmares of showering in icicles, my testicles solidified to stalactites. I was never, never, never warm, not even when my mother held me close after my father's programme to make a man of me. For she, poor soul, was too timid to show herself on my side, and as she held me, I felt the cold of her fear. And whenever I wished him dead, which was often, it was on her behalf as well as on my own. I knew nothing then of the relationship between my mother and my father. I learned later that she had much to tremble for on her own account, but as a small boy, I felt fear and cold as my sole right.

When I reached my tenth birthday, my bed-time was advanced, and I was up and having supper as my father came home from the shop. Often he was late and my mother would keep me up with her for company, and I knew, when we heard his key in the door, for her sake, to make myself scarce. But sometimes, he would come in through the back door, straight into the kitchen where we were sitting. He would be staggering, knocking himself on the sink-unit against the stove. 'Off to bed with you,' he hiccuped, and I weaved sharply out of his way to the door. But he was still shouting 'Off to bed with you,' when I was already in my room and I could only surmise that the order referred to my mother. And shortly afterwards, I would hear her occasional slipper on the stair, muffled by my father's heavy boots. What went on in their bedroom I could only conclude was punishment. I could hear my father's heavy breathing and it reminded me of the way he panted when he pounded my chest those cold mornings in the fields. I wondered whether he was making a man out of my mother too. I cried for her, knowing that if this were his cause, she had a lot further to go than I. Again I wished him dead, and I won-

54

dered, probably for the first time, why I did not kill him. But having entertained such a thought, I could not get it off my mind. I never considered the means of his dispatch. I was satisfied solely with the intent. Little boys have gone to sleep on stranger thoughts and I offer no apology. Nowadays, my last wakeful thoughts are less murderous, and I must confess, too guiltless to induce sleep. In my eleventh year, I slept like a log.

I don't know why I am telling you all this. The unease creeps upon me. Yet I cannot leave it for it is more to do with me than with my father. So I tell it you for my own sake, and not in any way to let you into secrets which I have no intention of divulging. I have already told you that he was a drunk, and although on his homecoming he reeked of beer, the meat smell was still overpowering, as if the beer fumes only served to bring out the flavour of his calling. I never remember him sober but I remember times, when in his cups, he could be kind. But after my tenth birthday, which seemed a turning point in my life, his intermittent kindness, such as it was, evaporated completely.

My birthday fell on their wedding anniversary, coincidence uneasy for celebration, and the idea was put about for a dinner-party, with a few close friends, theirs and mine. Which meant entirely theirs, for I had no friends, close or otherwise. But it meant presents and a late night, so I did not complain. My twelve years alone, and their fifteen together, the sentences running mainly concurrently, were to be celebrated in unison, and sensing the precarious state of their relationship, I rather hoped that in joint celebration my future happiness would in no way be conditioned by theirs.

There were to be a dozen of us altogether, married couples, six pockets, so I could reckon on half a dozen presents. Preparations started a few days before, with my father offloading a large cut of meat into the refrigerator. He pinched my mother's bottom as he closed the door. I remember it very clearly for, for some reason, I intended that he should pay for it. He went into the dining-room and poured himself an unending drink, and then another and another. Between each

55

glass, he would seek out my mother and pinch her with less than affection. I saw my mother wince and I told my father to stop it. He had never once been told what to do, and I expected the full treatment. But he didn't touch me. He staggered past the dining table and into the kitchen. I followed him because I feared he would take it out on my mother. But he brushed past her too, and went to the kitchen table where my mother had set out four large trifles, her speciality, which she had prepared for the celebration. And there and then, he unbuttoned his fly, and urinated into each one of them, taking a drunk's meticulous care to give each bowl its proper ration.

I stood and watched him. I marvelled less at what he was doing, than the sight of his member, which I realized I was seeing for the first time. I think my self-aversion was born at that moment, and I looked towards my mother with an overpowering envy. She was crushed and broken, it was true, but she was at least a woman. I watched her as my father, still unbuttoned, left the room, and saw her gather up the bowls one by one, and pour the contents down the sink, as if it was something my father did every day, and that she would clean up after him. I knew then, that one day I would kill him, and I began for the first time to think of the means.

I suppose they must have made it up, because when my birthday arrived there were four new trifles, twelve guests, six presents and the promise of an enjoyable if not a memorable celebration. I don't remember who was there, but I do recall an overwhelming smell of meat, since they were all in the trade, and until you got used to it, our dining-room smelt like an *abattoir* in full blast. I remember the conversation being punctuated with surnames, although they were all close friends, and I wondered at that a little. There was wine and my father was in charge of it, and each time he got up to circle the table and fill the glasses, keeping his own to the brim, my mother trembled. But miraculously he held it down. I remember that he was slightly more than jolly, but in the general atmosphere of celebration, he was nothing uncommon. Intemperance is in the eye of the beholder, and blurred or sharp according to the sobriety of that eye. I myself, I suppose, after two unaccustomed glasses saw a jollity without menace, but I was afraid to look at my mother, because if there were a danger, I knew that she could smell it, and that it would show on her face. My father suggested some dancing and he made his unsure way towards the gramophone. Everything was prepared, and he needed only to drop the needle, which he did, somewhere in the middle of a painful cry of rejected love. It was a slow tune, and as I see it now, meant as a warm-up to what he hoped might materialize, and had nothing to do with my twelfth birthday, and in all decency, even less with his anniversary. He grabbed at one of the Missuses as a sign of permission that couples could split, which they did, my mother hovering timidly on the edge of the room, terrified of two prospects, first of being asked to dance, and second, of not being asked at all. I remember toying with the idea of asking her myself, but I wasn't married to her, and it was hardly my duty. I was grateful that not only was she asked, but that two of the Misters awaited her favour. I watched them as they circled the room. I felt even then that my father was too close for comfort to the Missus of his choice, and I tried to attribute his wandering hands to his show of friendship. Again I was afraid to look at my mother. Her face was an accurate diviner and forecaster, and I dreaded what I might find there. The music stopped and my father clung to his woman for a while, and then, unwilling to let her go, dragged her over to the gramophone, and held her while he replayed the record. It saved the time of changing, and promised the same mood as before. I was bored, and what with repeats there was no indication that the record collection would soon be exhausted. When the song was over for the second time, my mother boldly crossed to the machine, and turned it off. 'George is bored,' she said. 'Let's all play a game.'

I was moved by her consideration, but resented being the focus of discontent. I knew my father would punish me for it. An extra run through the fields or a double shovel of snow on my bare back. It was summer still, but he would bide his time and remember, and I would have four long months to anticipate it. 'I don't mind,' I offered, but my mother had already suggested a game of blind man's buff, and even I thought that was rather childish. I was surprised that most of the grown-ups thought it a splendid suggestion, and one of their number, a Mister, was chosen to be blindfold. My mother did it herself with a table-napkin, while my father, sulking a little, poured the brandy. My mother turned the victim round three times and I noticed a look of extreme joy on her face, as if she were recalling her own childhood birthdays. There was much scuffling in the room to avoid the blinded figure, and when he caught one of the guests, there was much feeling up and down to identify her. My father, who until then, had been a sullen bystander, suddenly saw the possibilities in the game, and was impatient to have his turn. The blinded man in the centre still held on to his victim, and whether he knew her or not, he was taking his time to name her. So my father was restless, and threw out an unmistakable clue, and it would have been too obvious if the blind-fold had hesitated longer. He was obliged to name her, and she, having been identified, to take his place. But she refused, obviously preferring the role of potential catch. I offered to take her place. My mother was already blindfolding me, when I heard my father shout that he wanted a go. I was glad I couldn't see him, because I knew everybody was embarrassed by his behaviour, and I was still young enough to believe that if I shut my eyes, I was invisible. I heard him shout, 'It's my turn,' like a petulant child, and he seemed to be coming towards me. I knew that whatever happened, another punishment was added to the list, and the prospect of such a bleak winter appalled me. I felt the napkin torn from my eyes. I dared not open them, but I felt myself being pushed to one side. I heard a tittering embarrassed silence, and when I opened my eyes, I saw him bandaging himself in the middle of the room. My mother had withdrawn. She was obviously not going to play any more. The silence in the room was unpleasant and it took my father a while to revive the jollification. He did it by cavorting a little and making strange contortions with his body. The guests tittered, politely at first, and because they too preferred to get on with the party, because it would have been less embarrassing than breaking it up, laughed heartily and the mood was restored.

58

I watched my father and my hatred of him outweighed my embarrassment. I hoped fervently that he would die before winter. He had started to prowl around, taking his time with the catch. He wanted to prolong his fun. But when his hand landed on an obviously male worsted sleeve, he pounced backwards, as if he had touched nothing. He took his time, like a boxer dancing around his opponent, refusing to come into the fray, and eventually the guests tired of dodging something that wasn't there. Then my father suddenly darted across the room. My mother, who was hovering indifferently on the side, was a sitting duck for his lecherous hands, and he pounced on her, feeling her up and down, and I was astounded that out of all those women, he did not recognize the feel of his own wife. Not even the material of her dress, which he had probably never noticed, or the feel of her body, and I wondered when he had really touched her last. My mother sensed the danger of the situation, and vainly tried to get away, but my father was pawing at her, and in such delight and lechery, that it was patently obvious he had no notion who she was.

There was much laughter amongst the guests and I could have killed them all for it, but they were not to know of the consequences of my father's ignorance. My mother was trembling with fear, and I knew, as well as she, that on his discovery, he would punish her. The guests were laughing less now, curious as to how much more skin-pawing he needed to identify a body with which he had presumably slept for fifteen years, And as their curiosity grew, they became silent. My father, hearing the laughter trickle away, thought something amiss, and keeping one hand cupped on my mother's breast, with the other he tore away the blind-fold. I dared not look at him, but for my mother's sake, I had to. As for her, she hung her head, as if in shame of her identity. 'Jesus', I heard my father say, and then he looked round at his guests and was sobered into the realization of what he must have revealed of his state of matrimony. He caught sight of his hand on my mother's breast, and he flicked it away with disgust, as if he had touched a heap of dung. My mother slunk into the nearest chair, and one of the guests, with great presence of mind, put on a record. The music cheered the proceedings slightly, but it was obvious that welcome had been outstayed, and shortly afterwards, even before the record had been played out, the guests were taking their leave.

I went to bed as soon as they started to go. I had qualms about leaving my mother with him, but I needed desperately to be alone. I despised him, and I was afraid of what my hatred would lead to. I lay in bed and waited for their footsteps on the landing. I must have fallen asleep and when I awoke in the middle of the night, I could see the landing light still seeping through the bottom of my door. I wondered what they were still doing downstairs, and I dared to tip-toe across the landing to have a look. The living-room door was still open, and the light was still on, and I heard my mother weeping. I ran quickly downstairs, and as I entered the room, I knew by the sudden joy in my heart that my father was dead, and that I need not fear the winter. And indeed he sat there dead, as my mother said, from the heart, and I didn't know why she was weeping.

Neither do I know why I've told you all this. And you can believe it or not, I don't care. He's my father and I can tell you what I like about him. There he was, in the chair, dead from a heart-attack. Well, for what other reason should a man drop dead in the middle of the night? Anyway, I shall leave him there. He's interfered with my story and I don't want to refer to him again. But he was dead all right, and you can take it from me, and I'm pretty unprejudiced about these things, it was his heart. I don't know why I should bother to convince you. He's dead and that's the end of it, and I'll prove it by never mentioning him again.

I must try to get back to my story, and I can now, because he's not on my mind any more. I've just got to clean the place out after him.

7

I didn't realize what a mess my father left behind, so I cannot wholly guarantee that I shall never speak of him again, but if I do, it will only be by way of spring-cleaning, to clear a path for more relevant thought. So for the moment, I will leave him dead in that chair, from a heart-attack, I may add.

I went to school the following morning, again by the side route, and when I entered the common-room, the conversation ceased.

'Talking about me?' I said, with as much good humour as I could manage. 'Pray don't stop because I've arrived.' They did not respond. 'Any news of the Parsons affair?' I went on. I should not have shown myself so eager. 'It would be nice to know,' I said, gatecrashing their continued silence. 'After all, none of you is responsible for his work. I suppose we can take it for granted that he isn't coming back?'

'Would you take him back,' Miss Price asked, 'if you were headmaster?'

'I think it quite irrelevant what I would do,' I answered. I had no intention of starting a conversation with an arch-enemy. 'I'm sure you know his decision anyway,' I said. 'There's not much you don't know as far as he's concerned.'

She looked round the common-room for some support, but Miss Price was not well liked amongst the staff, and although no one would have dared to attack her, few would have rushed to her defence. Mr White, the neutral from Chemistry, quickly changed the subject and asked for confirmation of the date of the next parents' meeting. But since nobody knew or cared, that subject did not get off the ground. We were all glad when the bell rang, and I was grateful to go to my classroom. But on the way I remembered the new image of myself that I had resolved to present to the boys. I put a smile on my face and found it fatiguing. I half wished for Tommy's return and the spread of his story, so at least there would be something to deny. As I called the register, remembering this time to include Tommy's name, I realized that it was Tuesday, and a half-day for those not involved in games. I remembered my decision to buy some sundays for myself, and I decided to devote the afternoon to window shopping, if not to a little buying itself. I rushed through the register with excited anticipation. I looked up at the class and remembered the headmaster's warning to be on the lookout for strange behaviour amongst the boys.

'Anyone sullen here?' I said.

They stared at me blankly.

'Anyone with any problems?' I tried.

'What sort of problems, Sir?' They were confused by my line of questioning and they wanted to help me. 'D'you mean school problems?' one of them said.

'Any old problems,' I begged, like the rag and bone man, and they sat there, extrovert, uninhibited, problemless, screwing their faces into some semblance of neurosis that might answer to my request. 'Well, you're lucky,' I said. 'Now we can get on with some work.' I took my classes, and Mr Parsons's, gently through the morning. When I passed the boys in the corridor between lessons, I heard them whispering about me and marvelling at the sudden metamorphosis. I felt that perhaps I had gone too far, and should revert occasionally to my old unpleasant self, otherwise I would call suspicion upon me, and there was enough of that around without my inviting it. So I told them gruffly to be quiet and to get on to their classrooms, and I felt that they, as well as I, were relieved at the sniff of the old and known Verrey Smith.

When lunch-time came, I went straight to the bank to cash a cheque. I really had no intention of buying anything that afternoon, but I had to be prepared in case something caught my fancy, and I couldn't risk paying for it by cheque. I drew much more money than I had intended, and as I pocketed the notes I had a feeling that I had taken the first step on a decidedly hell-bent path, and that possibly I was making a great mistake, but that almost certainly, it was a path of intense enjoyment.

I took a bus to the outer part of town where the shopping, I had heard, was rather more exclusive, but not particularly for that reason, but that I was less likely to meet anyone there whom I knew. After about twenty minutes' ride, I got off at what looked like the start of a main street. The corner-shop window was a profusion of ladies' underwear and tho' I would dearly have loved to weave my eyes over the coloured laces and ribbons, I hurried past, strictly the man from the City, bent on buying something for his wife on their anniversary. I smiled at all the ladies who passed, hoping to give them the impression that a man bent on a mission such as mine could not help but love all women in his orbit, and I stoppped at each ladies' wear establishment window, in order to give them, as it were, a dress rehearsal. There were many ladies' shops, but they seemed to cater for the larger woman. I was in a residential area of genteel retirement, and I began to lose hope that I would find any shop that catered for the non-matron-like figure. And there, at the end of the shop parade, calling me with its creaking display sign, was the 'Femina Boutique', and its name seemed to answer all my requirements. I quickened my pace to the window, and I was not disappointed. Few items of clothing were on display, but every one of them I wanted for my own. I had already decided that I would go headlong into the shop and say whatever came into my mind, and not on any account to hover outside debating my approach. And so I made straight for the entrance, aggressively pushing the glass door. I was not to know that an electronic eye slid the doors open sideways, so that I almost fell into the shop into a staring circle of amused sales ladies. They had possibly seen the act many times before, and had never ceased to find it amusing, and they clamoured round the door for that purpose. It was not a good beginning. I recovered my calm, still smiling, and tried to direct my smile to just one assistant for, since there was no other client in the shop, it seemed that all of them were at my disposal. But none of them moved towards me, so I took a few steps into the centre of the shop. Perhaps they were waiting for me to look around. But I was too embarrassed to embark on a stock-taking without first having made my mission clear. I coughed, and all gave me their attention. 'I have a problem,' I said, not knowing specifically what the problem was, but sensing that it was an appropriate opening gambit. They gathered all four of them around me, used to problems, able to deal with them, full of solutions and sympathy. 'My wife has been ill, you see. She's been in hospital a long time.' There was a quartet trill of commiseration. 'But fortunately,' I went on quickly, 'she's coming out tomorrow, and I'd like to buy her a completely new outfit.' I was delighted with my invention, and so were they with their expected commission. They would be delighted to help, all four of them. 'What size is your wife?' said one.

Well fortunately, the blue chiffon was size-marked on its collar, at a fourteen. It fitted me perfectly for I am a slightly built man in spite of my father's gruelling training, and I must have stored the number in my mind for such an occasion as this.

'Fourteen,' I said. 'She's about the same height as me, but of course, she's got a better figure.' I had decided to be jolly with them. A jolly man is usually innocent.

'Shall we look at the dresses first?' another said. 'Does your wife have a favourite colour?'

'Black,' I said. Then I wondered why I had said it. My wife had come to hate black, thus black tended to be the colour of my hand-me-downs, but I was afraid to embark straightway on anything vivid. I had to give myself the least chance of detection. The girls held out one black dress after another, and it was all I could do to refrain from trying them on.

We were interrupted at this juncture by a little round lady who suddenly appeared from behind one of the curtains, and who gave me the impression she had been there all the time. She was smiling with the aftertaste of eavesdropping, dismissed the girls summarily, announcing that she would look after the gentleman herself. This made her, I suppose, the owner of the shop and she frightened me a little. From what she had overheard, she knew that after the weary week of ladies, just looking, I was indeed a serious customer. 'Very nice,' she said, pulling out a black indispensable loaded with sequins, obviously the most expensive of her collection and hardest to push.

'No,' I said firmly. I regretted the loss of my four giggling girls. I preferred not to be taken too seriously.

'No, my wife wouldn't like that at all.'

'Very good taste. Always in fashion, sequins,' she insisted, draping it across her short squat, ungainly body. 'Nice for a family function,' she persuaded. 'Not so well, she isn't, your wife? I'm sorry to hear,' she went on. 'Always troubles. But such a lucky woman. I should have a husband so interested. Believe me, Mister, I could put on a bridal gown' – I shuddered at the thought – 'would he notice? Ethel, he'd say, so where's my dinner? Ach, men,' she mused, 'such a lucky woman, your wife. She was very ill then? How long she in hospital?'

'My wife has been in a nursing home,' I said, upping my income a little. Ethel was duly impressed and taking her cue guided me over to a shrouded rail, where whispered her *haute couture* that could never be pushed to hospital clients. 'Is nice a nursing home,' she mused. 'People of account. But what difference,' she said. 'You should only have your health and strength. Very ill she was, your wife?'

Even if an illness was cured, it was clearly not beyond Ethel's range of discussion.

'My wife is very ill,' I confided. 'She will not get better. They are discharging her tomorrow because they can do no more.'

'Oy oy,' she keened. 'Such a life. I'm sorry, Mister. But you never know. The modern miracles. Who knows what they can do? Miracles they make nowadays. She got an incurable?'

She had to hear the word said. She herself could not pronounce it even in a whisper. It was an obscenity, titillating to hear from another's mouth, but for oneself, unutterable. So I gave it to her, loud and clear.

'My wife has cancer,' I said. 'It has gone too far.'

She gripped my arm. 'Mister,' she said confidentially, 'life is full of trouble. But we get over it. Believe me, we get over it.

God is good. But a man shouldn't be alone. Is not good a man with thank God his health and strength should be alone.' Ethel had already buried my good wife and put me squarely on the market. 'Excuse me, you don't mind I should ask.' She was no longer pulling out dresses. What was on her mind was certainly of greater importance. 'You're not a Jewish man,' she said, stating the worst so that my denial could only give her the greater pleasure, and I felt, indeed, that I couldn't possibly let her down. 'Of course I am,' I said.

She warmed to me and gave me a pang of conscience. 'In *shul* I don't see you.'

'No,' I said. 'I don't live around here.'

'Is far you live?'

Her indirect method of questioning was tiring me a little, so I gave her an address in the most elegant quarter of town, and I knew by her stunned silence that Ethel was impressed. So now she knew, or thought she knew, my religion, and what with the nursing home and my address, she had some inkling of my income. Only one thing she didn't know, and that was my status in society. I could have answered her next question without her prompting.

'You make a good living?' She was indirect again. 'In the properties, I suppose.'

'No,' I said. 'I'm a doctor.'

She smiled. I had everything. Money, position, education, and I saw her shift me on to the top line in her books. I hastened to add that I was a surgeon – might as well go the whole hog, I thought – and that I was known as Mister.

'Oh Doctor,' she said, notwithstanding. 'Such a lovely profession. You should only keep your health and strength.'

'Now about my wife,' I said, bringing her back to the present situation.

'Ach, your poor wife,' she said. 'So why in her condition must she wear black? Something gay she needs. Flowers. Flowers are in this year. They're all wearing them, all the young girls. Even me, Doctor,' she laughed, pointing to the undulating spread of red dahlia across her torso, 'and believe me, I'm no chicken.'

But I insisted on black, and withdrew from the first rail a silk dress that had held my eye ever since I had entered the shop. She took it from me and held it at arm's length. 'Very nice,' she said. 'Very feminine.' She draped it over her front, and managed in the gesture to drain the garment of any vestige of femininity it once had. I took it from her and, unable to resist it, put it against my own body and walked over to the full-length mirror. I could see her bewildered face in the reflection. I realized my mistake, and hastily explained that I was trying it for height.

'She's rather tall, you see,' I said weakly.

'A tall woman,' Ethel marvelled, from the limit of her fifty-nine inches. 'Such trouble I should have. But it takes all sorts, Doctor,' she said.

'I'll have this one,' I said, getting back to business.

She took it from me and examined it. 'A mistake you haven't made,' she said. 'Very nice. Mind you, is not what I call a good buy. Is not very expensive, but then, is not expected to last like for instance, this one.' She was at the sequins again.

'I'm not buying for durability,' I reminded her.

'Still,' she said, unwilling to acknowledge her *faux-pas*, 'a good dress you never throw away. Now what about a nice coat. Phoebe,' she called over. 'Forward, Phoebe. Model the coats for the doctor.'

Phoebe tried on one coat after another. I knew that all of them would have looked better on me. I fell for a black one with an astrakhan collar and cuffs and, without bothering to check on the price, I asked for it to be wrapped. Although I was impatient to investigate the underwear department, I thought it politic to leave that choice in Ethel's ham-fisted hands, stressing first, that my wife liked frills, ribbons and bright colours in her lingerie, and giving her an idea of what I was prepared to spend. Phoebe was dispatched to make a selection, and she returned it for my inspection. I had to take a hold on myself as she laid out the frilly petticoat and mesh tights, and when I saw the lace panties, I fairly lost all control. I told her quickly to wrap it all up, and to total my bill. Accounts was Ethel's department, and she added it up with relish.

I asked Phoebe to pack each item separately, for that seemed to me a more hideable proposition than one large package. Ethel checked the bill many times over, and to my surprise and probably to hers, it amounted to far less than I had feared, and I resolved to go on shopping expeditions more regularly, to boutiques in various districts, armed with sufficient cash, and the woeful tale of my moribund spouse. Life looked infinitely pleasing, and I smiled at Ethel and felt sorry for her ugliness.

'Come again, Doctor. Don't be strange. A lovely selection I always have. Every season something new.' She bit her lip suddenly as she realized her gaffe. 'For a friend, perhaps,' she added quickly. 'Where is there a lady, I'm asking you, who doesn't like from time to time a new outfit. You like you should leave me your address. I should let you know of end-of-season sales.' Poor Ethel was unwilling to let me go, having sensed that in my given situation, she was unlikely to see me again. I shook my head, sadly I hoped.

'All right,' she said. 'So no dresses. You come sometimes. A little chat with an older woman. It helps sometimes, believe me. You have troubles, Doctor. But don't we all have troubles? Come, come. Don't be strange.'

I smiled at her, and then I did a most inappropriate thing. I felt sorry that I had deceived her, and it was probably to give the lie to all I had told her. I pinched her bum, and I left the shop. As I went through the electronic door, careful this time not to participate in my leaving, I heard her saying to Phoebe, 'Not like a Yiddishe gentleman. Not a bit,' and I wondered whether or not I had conned her.

I was impatient to get home. I toyed with the idea of a taxi. I could hide myself more happily inside a taxi than I could on public transport, and I dared not risk any encounter, laden as I was with an orange parcel that screeched the purple legend of 'Femina Boutique'. On both sides too, so no concealment was possible. I hailed a passing cab and gave him the address of a street not too far from my home, from which I hoped to make my way through the back lanes unseen. I hoped that my wife like the good neighbour she was, would be doing her duty by

Mrs Johnson next door, so that I would have the house to myself in which to try on my wares. Inside the taxi, I could not resist the temptation to take a peep at what I had bought, and in spite of my excitement, or perhaps because of it, it was hard to stifle the creeping thoughts of that rotten father of mine. One day, I shall tell you about him, not everything of course, but all that you need to know. Not now, though, because I don't want to interrupt that journey home with my wardrobe, and my ecstatic anticipation of trying it on. Because even on reflection, and in the telling, I can experience once again, that joy of becoming myself. And this joy, and its supreme moments were worth the gnawing irritation of its inevitable concomitant.

I had my fare ready so that I could slip out of the taxi unobserved, and I let myself into the mercifully empty house, still hiding my gear under my coat and feeling like a housebreaker. For although in my sundays I felt at home and completely identified with myself, when I was dressed otherwise, my study, my home and all its tangible furnishings were suddenly strange to me. They were the property of someone else, someone other than my real self. I had never any doubts as to which one of us was real. It was in my school clothes that I was playing a part. In fact, for a good ninety per cent of my waking life, I was living a lie. So it was not surprising that, as I crept through the dining-room up to my study, my sundays under my arm, and already in my mind a woman, I felt like an intruder, with the same kind of fear that a burglar must experience when there is the odd chance that he won't get away with it.

I locked my study door and laid the clothes out on the bed. I wanted to take my time, and to examine each item hollow, the better to savour the effect when I put them on. As dear Ethel had said, 'Like nothing it looks on a hanger, Doctor. Take it. Try it. You don't like it. So bring it back. Something else perhaps you fancy. I don't believe in an unsatisfied customer. How else should I keep in business? Listen Doctor,' I recalled her saying, 'a satisfied customer always comes back.'

Not this one, dear Ethel, I thought. It's new pastures for me next time. And I had a frightful vision of entering a boutique the other side of town, and delivering my tale of woe to the *patronne*, who turned out, after a little closer scrutiny to be none other than a slightly ageing Ethel. 'So long your wife takes to die?' I heard her say. Again I felt guilty for my story, not on my wife's behalf, but because I felt sorry for Ethel's gullibility.

I started on my make-up, not too fastidiously this time, for I was anxious to try on my clothes. Then I stripped completely, and started with the underwear. I don't expect you to understand my feelings. You probably think I am perverted, or if generous, you will allow me insane. But I am neither of these. I am myself, with possibly a greater difficulty in trapping my own identity than you have. In any case, I care not what you think, but had you seen me that day, fully dressed in my new clothes, you would have envied me, and wished, man or woman, that you could be likewise.

I dressed completely, without once looking in the mirror. And then I hesitated before the final confrontation. And when I braved it, I gasped. Every item fitted superbly, and I knew that I was beautiful. I stood looking at myself for a long time, occasionally lifting up the dress and coat, to delight in the colours of the frills underneath. I drew up a chair, and sat opposite the mirror, crossing my legs to reveal discreetly the breaking of the black. Then I stood up and marvelled at the drama of the colour. Black was a colour full of suggestion and promise. It was the colour of my own self, my facsimile. I wondered whether I had been aware of it in the boutique. Why indeed had I insisted on black? And then I realized, that somewhere along the line, consciously or otherwise, I had made the decision to go to Mr Johnson's funeral in drag.

8

It was becoming quite obvious that I had neglected to visit Mrs Johnson since the day her husband died. The post-mortem had been performed and I was publicly in the clear. The funeral was to take place within the week, and I had already told my wife that due to pressure of work in school and Mr Parsons's absence – I said nothing about its cause – it would be impossible for me to take the time off. All the more reason, she supposed, that I should call and pay my respects. I waited for an evening of the mid-week, when I felt that other people would be present because, much as I was excited by the memory of Mrs Johnson, I did not particularly wish to be alone with her. On the other hand, if Tommy chose to open his mouth, it would be preferable if no one else were in ear shot. It was a risk either way. But I had no choice. I had to go and see her, otherwise my continued absence would be considered an effrontery. So after school on the Thursday, I knocked at her door. I think Tommy must have been its permanent sentry. He opened within minutes of my knocking, and the hostility in his eyes was fixed, as if he'd been expecting me. I raised my hand to rub his hair, as a gesture of sympathy, but quickly had second thoughts, since he might attribute to such a move the natural concern of a father. 'How are you, Tommy?' I said, trying a man-to-man approach. 'Are you looking after your mother?'

'Huh,' he said insolently, and once again I dreaded his return to school.

'Pardon, Tommy?' I said.

But he made no answer. I made my way to the living-room.

'Aren't you going to have a bath, then?' he sneered at me. I had to get things straight, and I went over to him and squatted down to his level, a position I would never have dreamed of assuming in the classroom. But I had to reprimand this boy, and at the same time remain sympathetic, and I reckoned that my position was a neat compromise. 'Now look, Tommy,' I said. 'I know you're upset. It's a terrible thing for a boy to lose his father.'

'Huh,' he said again, and I decided to let it pass.

'But at the same time,' I said, rising to a standing position as my sympathy waned. 'There is no need to be rude, to anybody, that is, not only to your form teacher. Do not forget, Tommy, that I am, after all, your teacher, and though I am willing to help you in every way, and to make allowances for you in your work and behaviour, there are, and never will be allowances made for insolence. Now do you understand?'

He scuffed his toe-caps with his heels. 'My father isn't dead,' he challenged me, 'and I wish 'e was.'

'Were. Subjunctive,' I corrected him, and I heard the echo of my own childhood wish and wondered whether he could wish it hard enough, as hard as I had myself, to bring it about. I am a firm believer in the evil eye, but it is unnerving to think that the eye may be focused on a mistaken identity, and the need to clarify my position, as far as Tommy was concerned, became more and more urgent. I squatted down again. 'Look, Tommy,' I said, 'I am not your father. Get that absolutely clear. You know Mrs Verrey Smith,' I said. 'You know we've been married for seventeen years. That's a lot more than your mother and father. Yet we have no children. And d'you know why, Tommy,' I whispered, hoping thereby to gain his sympathy. 'Between you and me, Tommy, I cannot have children. It's as simple as that.'

He stared at me with disgust. 'It's 'er wot can't 'ave them,' he said. 'Mrs Verrey Smith. Everyone knows that.'

I wanted to strangle him. There was I, squatted, offering my infertility to a ten-year-old kid, and he threw it back in my face. Moreover, his logic told him that my wife's sterility was reason enough for me to sire elsewhere. 'That's why,' he continued, 'you 'ad it off with my Mum.'

I was horrified more at his language than at the matter of

his words, and all I could do, short of killing him, was simply to deny it. 'It's not true, Tommy,' I said. 'Your mother and father had a quarrel. You heard it. And your father accused your mother of certain things, and your mother got so angry that, just to annoy him, she told him he was right. But she only did it because she was angry,' I pleaded, and the whole sorry tale sounded so hollow and lacking in truth, I couldn't really expect Tommy to believe it.

'Anyway,' he said, and I caught the sob in his voice. 'I know 'e wasn't my Dad, but I miss 'im.'

I took his head in my hands. To hell with how he construed it. The boy was in pain, and no one could have done less than simply to acknowledge it. 'I'll go and see your mother,' I said.

Mrs Johnson was alone. It seemed that she had not moved from the position in which I had last seen her. She looked up as I came in and smiled weakly. I went straight over to her. 'How are things?' I said.

She shrugged her lovely shoulders. 'I was wondering why you haven't been,' she said. 'Tommy keeps talking about you. He knows. He heard everything. And he won't believe it when I tell him it isn't true.' Then, as a complete *non-sequitur,* 'The cremation is on Thursday.'

'You have to forgive me for my absence,' I said. 'But we have Mr Parsons away from school, and I've been saddled with all his work. I'll come and see you in the evening. Will Tommy be going?'

'No, he'll be staying with his aunt, Jack's sister,' she added.

I wondered how that lady fitted into Tommy's new family tree.

'It's best for him to get away,' I said limply. 'What are you going to do? After the funeral, I mean. Are you going to stay here?' I tried to hide the persuasion in my voice, but she'd caught it.

'D'you think I ought to leave?'

I detected a distinct pleading in her voice, a helplessness, as if she were placing the decision for her whole future into my hands, and as if to confirm this, she laid her hand on my knee.

Now I want to make a few things clear at this point. I had nothing to do with that initial move. My knee just happened to be there, but it was she who put her hand on it, and a woman's hand on a man's knee, and a bereaved hand at that, can be the beginning of many things. And of course, my knee trembled. I defy any man to keep a stiff upper knee in such circumstances. She took it as response, as well she might. 'D'you think I ought to leave?' she said again, with more of a challenge this time.

In response, I placed my hand on her knee, not crosswise over hers, for that, I intuitively felt, would be asking for trouble, but laying as a parallel, a position slightly more thoroughbred, and still, though marginally so, excusable by affection. I should, of course, have taken the precaution of occupying my other hand, in my pocket perhaps, but since it was free, she took it, and placed it, quite logically I suppose, given as she was to symmetry, on her other knee. There was now no longer any need for conversation, for there was already enough between us, and it had nothing to do with love. I knew that for my part at least, it was lust. Nothing more, nothing less. And I assumed that for her it was likewise, prompted perhaps by a need to confirm herself once again amongst the living. But all this is irrelevant, since lust does not concern itself with motivation. On reflection, it is of course possible, that both of us, having been accused, thought that we might as well be guilty. And so our hands wandered, detached from all thought, manoeuvring a gradual state of undress.

And it was thus that Tommy, arriving slippered on the edge-to-edge, found us, fumbling, writhing and apart.

I looked at him, not immediately connecting the horror on his face with my own state of partial undress. And then I saw his mother's skirt hoiked up to her thigh, and I thought she was disgusting.

'You're filthy and rotten,' he shouted at us both, 'and I'm going to tell my Dad.' He drew his breath, stunned by his own horrible confusion. 'I'm going to tell everybody,' he screamed. 'Everybody. I'll shout it in the street.'

I clapped my hand over his mouth. 'You don't understand,'

was all I could say. 'Your mother was overwrought.' I realized that at one time I had offered that plea for his mother before.

'Overwrought,' he sobbed, and I found it hard to stifle a feeling that he couldn't even spell the word. 'You're always saying that. But I'll tell everyone. I mean it. You're just dirty and rude. 'Er too,' he nodded in the direction of his overwrought mother, who by this time, had lowered her skirt.

'You're not old enough to understand,' she said.

'I don't care. You're rude and filthy, and I'm old enough to understand that, and I don't care if you are my father, or my teacher,' he was screaming again, 'I'm going to tell them all in school, and the headmaster, too. You filthy rude things.' His dearth of vocabulary infuriated him, and knowing my penchant for synonyms, he felt bound, out of spite if nothing else, to repeat himself again in the same manner. 'Filthy and rude, both of you.'

He went over to the door, out of reach, and he gave himself a moment's pause. Breathless with rage, he stared at the floor. 'A pair of fucking pigs, both of you.'

His mother crossed over to him, no longer the accused, and slapped him roundly across the face. 'I don't know where you learn such language,' she said, 'unless you pick it up at school.' She turned on me with a look of hatred, and the sudden alliance between the two of them, frightened me. Tommy began to cry, and she too, burying their faces in each other's arms, and I knew I had to get out of there, and leave them both to their own explanations, their own mutual forgiveness. But there was one small practical point. Their entwined bodies were blocking the door. As I walked across the room, I noticed that my trousers were still unbuttoned. With one hand, I made myself respectable, while with the other, I tapped her on the shoulder. 'Excuse me, please,' I said, and I edged my way between them and the door.

Once outside in the street, I felt as if I had just come out of a cloakroom, and I intended to give it no more importance than just that. I knew I'd left a mess behind, but I didn't care, because for some reason, I felt that neither of them would ever see me again. I suddenly felt very weary with my present way of life, and I knew that some decision had to be made to change it radically, though what change, or how to engineer it, I had no idea. But I knew that my life could not continue in its pretence much longer, and despite my depression, there was a certain excitement in the thought that some change was bound to come about, even, as I convinced myself, without my own participation. I had thoughts of going home and once more trying on my new sundays, but pangs of that old father of mine, blunted the edge of that anticipation. All in all, I was lethargic with depression. I turned back to look at the Johnson house, and had it been on fire, it would not have moved me. I gave a fleeting thought to the two broken people inside and was furious with their gross interference with my life. I looked at my own house, but that too held nothing for me, save the delights of the 'Femina Boutique', and that, after all, was something, in spite of the rage that my father was pumping inside me. I grabbed the railings hard, trying to throttle his rude ghost, and then I felt myself weeping.

I am almost ashamed to write that word, for I am not a man given to tears. And still I have no notion of why I cried. I remember only that I wanted to rid myself of Mrs Johnson and her son, of my poor joyless and childless Joy, of my mother and father too, and of all the loud unhappiness that I had tunnelled into other people's lives. I'll say that word again. I wept uncontrollably, and I don't give it to you as a plea in mitigation. I'm a bastard really, and a sentimental one at that.

9

That last piece of confession took a great deal out of me, and it has taken some time to recover my old rotten self. There is not a great deal that is gentle in my nature, but occasionally it gets the upper hand. Not that I resent it. I simply do not know how to deal with it. Friends, such as I have, have told me to let it take its course, that I am a better man than I allow myself to be. But I dare not give way to whatever kindness is within me, for the virtue destroys my defences. In truth, I do not like myself very much. That too, is a defence I suppose, for it makes pointless any attack you may wish to make on me. You are right. I am rotten, and deserve no one's concern, and if at any time I should be repentant of my behaviour, I beg you to ignore it. Remorse would be a lapse in me, as much as kindness. I hope we are now on the old footing again, and I can go back to my sorry tale.

On Thursday, the day of the funeral, it was raining. As a child, holding my mother's hand, and seeing a funeral in the rain, she would tell me that the world was weeping for the one who had died. So that when a cortège passed under a blazing sun, it was a devil going to his own, and the world was smiling. I never quite rid myself of this conviction, and occasionally it was shaken, as it was on that Thursday, when I couldn't understand how anyone could mourn the passing of a man like Johnson, who, when dead, looked uncommonly like my own father. I hoped it would clear up by the afternoon, not so much as a more fitting salute to Mr Johnson's obsequies, but because I feared spoiling my new sundays, which were already laid out on my study couch in preparation for my first and probably fatal sortie.

That morning, my wife and I breakfasted together, an uncommon occurrence, and without any apparent design. I was relieved to hear that she was spending the whole day at Mrs Johnson's, and would go to the funeral from there. That would give me the privacy and the time to change my clothes in my study. I made a point of informing my wife yet again, that I would not be attending the funeral, owing to pressure of work, and that I would meet her at the Johnson house in the evening.

I laid my plans with infinite care. I could not afford to be discovered, certainly not before the sortie itself, and I cared little what happened afterwards. For some reason, I felt that post-production planning was not necessary.

I went to school by the back route and on arriving, went straight to the Cloth's study to ask permission to attend Mr Johnson's funeral in the afternoon. It was a slight risk, but I couldn't get the afternoon off for any other reason. It was a request that could hardly be refused by a man of God, and he was quick to grant it, and with his blessing, too, that I was to be party to a Christian gesture. As I was leaving, he called me back, and again I had the sinking feeling that I had been discovered. 'I think perhaps I shall put in an appearance myself,' he said. 'The late Mr Johnson was a great asset to our Parent Teacher Association. It would be a gesture to his widow. So I shall see you there, Verrey Smith.' He turned back to his desk. 'An unhappy occasion,' he muttered, 'but in the midst of life, Mr Verrey Smith. You know how it is.' I left the room. I had not in any way prepared myself for this eventuality and I was a little worried as to how to accommodate the Cloth's presence at the funeral. Yet it did not occur to me to abandon my sortie as a woman. In fact, the promised attendance of the Reverend Richard Baines added to my excitement. If I could con Baines, I could con anybody.

During the course of the morning I had occasion to go to the stationery room to replenish my stock. On my way there I had to pass Baines's study, and I was surprised to find Mr Parsons standing outside in the attitude of a small unruly pupil awaiting his strapping. An encounter, and a dialogue of sorts, was unavoidable. I slowed down as I reached him, and for some reason stared at his fly, expecting, I suppose, to find him unbuttoned. But he stood there, respectable and very much on his dignity.

'You heard about it, I suppose,' he said.

'Yes, the Cloth told us on Monday. I'm sorry about it, Parsons.'

'Mr Parsons,' he said, catching the accusing implication of my mode of address. 'I am not guilty. I have nothing to be ashamed of. I have come to clear my name.'

I felt like giving him a sweeping brush for all the good it would have done him. 'You'll have to have a pretty good story, then,' I said. Such sympathy as I had had for the man was rapidly waning. 'A boy doesn't get into such a state for nothing.'

'It's his word against mine,' Parsons said.

'There's more than his word,' I ventured. 'There were apparently other little boys.'

'You've been brainwashed, Verrey Smith,' he said. 'You and probably the rest of them. I've got a fiancée in Brighton. We're getting married soon. What would I be wanting with little boys?'

'You'd better keep your defence for inside,' I said nodding at the Cloth's door. I noticed Parsons's eyes for the first time. They watered but not with sorrow. There was something quite disgusting about them. I had no doubt that Parsons made his afternoon forays to the back of the maintenance shed, and there indulged his perversion. I was as sure of it as I was of my own hobby, and the moisture in his eyes was something I had often caught in my own, in moments of extreme sexual pressure and frustration. 'Look, Parsons,' I said, 'I don't care what filthy business you get up to, but I do care if it involves innocent little boys.' I could have been the Cloth himself talking, and when I heard echoes of that raspberry voice in my own, I was silent, and felt slightly ashamed. I put my arm on Parsons's shoulder. 'Anyway,' I said, 'it's a rotten business for you, and I wish you luck with him.'

The Cloth had opened his door. He had obviously heard my last remark, and he saw my hand on Parsons's shoulder.

'It seems that my little homily of last Monday did not entirely reach home,' he said.

I kept my hand on Parsons's shoulder.

'Such cameraderie,' he spat the word, eyeing my affectionate hand, 'does little credit to you, Verrey Smith, and perhaps in the process of spring-cleaning this school, it would be as well to look into your own – er – records.'

I thought for a moment he was going to say wardrobe, and I smiled with relief.

'You have an uncommon sense of humour, Verrey Smith,' he said tartly, 'a humour which often leads to the back of the maintenance shed, and other such dubious locations. I am ready for you now, Parson,' he went on hurriedly, 'and you would do me a favour, Mr Verrey Smith, if you returned to your classes.'

My hand was left in mid-air as he wheeled Parsons round by the tips of his fingers and into his study. I felt the situation was getting quite beyond me, but I didn't care for the consequences. All that concerned me was that nothing should interfere with my afternoon's debut.

I had been dealing with Mr Parsons's classes for most of the morning, and after the break was the first opportunity I had of taking my own. What confronted me when I entered my classroom was something so entirely unexpected and seemed part of the general conspiracy to thwart my afternoon's pleasure. A large wreath stood leaning against the blackboard, and for a moment I felt it was for myself, placed as it was against my inalienable property.

'It's for Mr Johnson,' the back row chorused. 'We all paid for it, Sir.'

'That's very nice indeed,' I said without much pleasure, feeling that an inordinate amount of fuss was being made over Mr Johnson's demise. First, the headmaster's threatened attendance at the burial, and now this wreath, not to mention the fact that I was using the funeral as a funfair of my very own.

'We thought you'd take it with you, Sir,' Tindall said. 'Say it's from us.'

Another complication. I had to sort it out right away. 'I

80

think it would be nicer if one of you were to take it himself, as a representative of the class.'

'Let's vote, let's vote,' they shouted, excited at the possibility of some diversion.

'I doubt whether this is a question for voting,' I said. 'I think it would be as well to draw a name out of a hat.' This method, I thought, would take a lot longer and pass the morning without undue frustration. Moreover, by the voting method, there was a sporting chance that one of Tommy's closer friends would be chosen, and after our last encounter, I couldn't risk exposing a pupil to Tommy's confidences. The offer of the hat method appealed to their natural gambling instincts, and they set about writing their names on pieces of paper happily torn from their exercise books. I walked round the class as they each laid their claim, and noticed that most of them were writing in their very best hand as if the prize were a reward for calligraphy.

I decided to use a satchel as our bran-tub, and I went round collecting the papers. When I reached Tindall, I noticed that he put a handful of his signatures into the bag, and I made him retrieve all of them as a penance for his attempted cheating. It took me a little while to subdue his violent reaction, and coward that I am, I called upon the whole class to condemn him, because it was, after all, not wholly in their interest that Tindall should be represented a dozen times. The class turned on him and they settled the matter between them.

I took it upon myself to make the draw, for I trusted nobody. I stood in the middle of the classroom, in view of them all, and shook the satchel for a good mélange. I allowed the nearest boy to hold the bag while I fumbled around inside it. Everybody, with the possible exception of Tindall, was in a state of thorough enjoyment, myself included. What the hell, I thought. Why shouldn't we get a bit of fun out of old Mr Johnson. He'd caused me enough trouble by dying. I fumbled in the bag, longer than was necessary, in order to prolong the suspense, and then I withdrew a crumpled piece of paper and returned with it to my desk in order to lay it out with ceremony. It held the name of Michael Roberts, in his best writing, and it belonged to the smallest boy in the class, fortunately from my point of view, a close friend of nobody's leave alone Tommy's. I declaimed the winner and the name was greeted with roars of disapproval. ' 'S too big for 'im, Sir. 'E won't be able to carry it.'

'I can, so there,' little Roberts squeaked. The excitement croaked in his voice, and they laughed at him. Poor Roberts was close to tears, an appropriate demeanour, I felt, for wreath-hauling, and I proposed he should leave right away, while grief, whatever its cause, was still upon him.

' 'E doesn't know the 'ouse, Sir,' one of the boys tried again.

'I do, so there,' Roberts croaked, as he came up to the black-board to collect his delivery.

It was indeed mightily large for him, and he tried to conceal that he had difficulty in manoeuvring it. He held it in front of him, like a shield, and because of his lack of height and the wreath's length, he was obliged to hold it high, and the strain on his thin little arms must have been appalling. I gave him the address, though he swore that he knew it, and I patted him ever so gently on his back. He put all his meagre strength into leaving the classroom with dignity, holding the wreath high and before him, like a lame Olympic runner. When he had gone, the class crowded round the windows to see him through the playground. After a while, he appeared, struggling with his charge, trying all manner of positions in which to carry it. Then half-way across the playground, he stopped, as if inspired. Then quickly he hung the wreath around his neck and belted across the yard as fast as his matchsticks would carry him. Behind him, he left a coloured trail of pocket-money tributes and I dreaded to think what would be left of the wreath by the time he got it to the Johnson house.

Shortly afterwards, the bell rang for the end of the morning, and I went back to the staff-room to deposit my books. I had plenty of time. The funeral wasn't until two o'clock. An hour and a half to go. I had generously calculated an hour to put on my sundays, so I dawdled a little with trivial chat to other staff members. By about twelve-thirty they had all returned to the common-room, and it was a full and chatty house, when the door swung open and Parsons, dishevelled and overwrought, his upper lip spurting blood, blazed on the threshold, eyeing us all with such hatred, I could not help but admire him. My first thought was to question who had been his adversary, but when I saw Miss Price gather herself to her lisle feet, and almost bolt past him out of the door, I knew that Florence Nightingale was on her way to the Cloth.

'What happened?' I said. It seemed I was the only one with tongue enough to talk to him.

'He gave me the push,' Parsons said, without moving, 'and I did the same for him. He's not looking too pretty himself,' he said. 'I just came to collect my things. I'm not going to fight it,' he said, reaching into his locker. 'I don't stand much of a chance. But I didn't do it, no matter what any kid says. I've got a fiancée in Brighton. I don't need any niggers in the wood-pile.'

I could have hit him then, but I turned away, as did the rest of the staff as he ranted on into his locker.

'I've got a fiancée in Brighton,' he kept repeating, as if a fiancée in Brighton, or indeed any other place, precluded any dirty business elsewhere. Why, I myself had a wife, but there was little point in quoting my spouse to Tommy while my hot hand fumbled up his mother's skirt.

'Well, you'd better go to Brighton, hadn't you?' Mr Gardiner suggested.

'I've got a fiancée in Brighton,' Parsons said again, as if that were a reason for *not* going there.

'So you keep on saying,' Mr Gardiner said wearily.

By now, Parsons had emptied his locker. His arms were full of exercise books and the odd textbook amongst the piles. He placed them all on the long table, then systematically took each one, textbooks included, and tore them into pieces, casting the shreds like confetti over the common-room floor. We all stared at him, but no one made a move to stop him. We were the sort of crowd that throughout history have indifferently watched the burning of books. One by one, they all left, and I remained for a while, while he shed his demoniac rage. 'You poor old sod,' I said, as he tore up the last exercise book. 'You'd better go and have yourself seen to.'

He turned on me as if he would lay me low as well, but I managed to get out of the common-room before he reached me.

In the corridor, I ran into Miss Price, hot from the Cloth, bearing a bloodied swab in her hand, and I had the feeling she'd lost her virginity.

I went into my house by the back door, trembling with excitement. I had almost an hour left in which to change, and the house was all to myself and my privacy. I went straight to my study and peered through the net curtains. A great black hearse stood outside the Johnson door, the coffin already inside. Over it lay a mound of wreaths, and on the pavement, the overflow. Amongst them, I caught sight of Tommy's form's contribution. It was, as I had feared, sadly depleted, but there was more grief in the cold wire armature of the circle, than in all the flowers that had stubbornly held their form.

I dropped the curtain, and on turning back into the room, I saw a letter that had been pushed under my door. It was my wife's habit to deliver my mail in this fashion, and on entering my study on my return from school, it had become automatic with me to take a high step over the threshold so as not to damage any correspondence I might have received. I had seen the letter when I had first entered the room, lying under my raised foot, but recognizing the postmark, I had pretended it wasn't there. Now, with my back to the window, it stared at me and could not be denied. Over the course of relating this narrative, and indeed long before, I have received many similar letters, all with the same threatening Irish stamp, usually franked with some Emerald Isle jingoism. I delay opening them, for I know the message inside. It is always the same. The letters are from my mother. I haven't spoken of her before, except in passing, because I've given you enough to put up with that rotten father of mine, without burdening you with my mother as well. But I should tell you that since my mother remarried some years ago, she has had but two words to say to me, and they arrive regularly, once a week, under those green stamps. The message never varies, like a monotonous litany.

She married an Irish churchgoer, with all the trimmings. Massing and confessing together, she found herself once more in the church. Well, that was her problem and I rather resented the fact that each week I was the recipient of her green stamp neurosis. I picked the letter up. Even now, after years of weekly missives I nourished the hope that perhaps one day her theme would allow itself a slight variation. And on this day, which had already been fraught with incident, and threatened much more, the letter that I opened was indeed other than the rest. I spread it out on my desk. She wrote in purple ink. Always, for that was the colour of her sermon. 'CONFESS, CONFESS,' it read, as it had shouted in capitals once a week over the past twelve years. And then, almost as a postscript, she had made the additional plea of, 'My son.' I was moved by this sudden appellation, seeing myself gloriously in my filial role, and she in her maternal, but then it occurred to me, that she might so totally have joined the ranks of the church, that she saw herself as a priest, and myself as one of her flock. Was she coming closer to me, or drifting apart? The codicil to her message could have meant either. I decided that either way she must be going off her rocker, and I gave her letter the same treatment as I had given all the others. I took my red pencil which screamed against her purple and wrote BALLS in large capitals across her plea. Then I screwed it up into the waste-paper basket, and tried to forget about it. Over the years, it had taken me the better part of the week to get her admonishment out of my mind, and barely erased, yet another would arrive. As if I needed any reminder of my rotten father.

My new sundays lay on the couch, and it was all I could do to recapture my excitement. Ignoring my mother, or my father for that matter, was no way of getting rid of them. That was becoming abundantly clear. If they would not pass out of my life, then I would have to disappear from theirs. And once again I had the feeling that a radical change was due in my existence. The thought gave me new hope, and I started to undress. I took off all my clothes, and after washing, put on my dressing-gown. I felt that it was the last male garment I was to wear for a long time. Then I started on my maquillage. Although it was going well, I took my time. My hand occasionally shook with excitement, so that I had to re-do my eye make-up a number of times. Even so, I was finished early, and all that remained was my clothing.

As I put on the first garments, the frilly petticoat and panties, my excitement gave way to fear, and I kept crossing to the window and lifting the curtain, as if in continuous dress-rehearsal for what had now become a dreaded debut. I trembled as I put on my stockings, and ham-fistedly hooked them to my belt. Occasionally I thought of foregoing the whole business. In my anguish I was aware that my sortie had assumed the status of an imperative, and that perhaps it might even be without pleasure. I was terrifyingly near ready. All that remained was the dress. I hesitated before putting it on, because I knew somehow that it was the final commitment. I looked at my open wardrobe, the trousers, jackets and shirts, my life's fiction. And I knew that whatever happened that day, that forged part of me had gone for ever. It was a terrifying revelation.

When I was fully changed and bewigged, I confronted my reflection and found it undeniably fool-proof. I was slightly disappointed. I had hoped perhaps for a loop-hole of give-away. I had hoped perhaps to run a greater risk. But as I looked at myself, I knew that without doubt I was going to get away with it. My excitement was mixed with a slight vexation of spirit.

Once again I looked through the net curtain. People were coming out of the Johnson house, Mrs Johnson amongst them, supported by my wife in her black do-gooding gear, and no doubt thoroughly enjoying herself. They all piled into cars that had meanwhile arrived, and I waited for them to drive off before taking to the streets myself. I was full of confidence, so much so, that I did not hesitate to use my front door for my exit. The street was empty, and I was able to pass down it without encounter. The crematorium was only a few streets away. When we had first considered buying our house, I had objected to this factor, but my wife, being a woman poor in imagination, had found this no adequate reason to look else-where. So as the crow flew, we were one minute from the chimney, but on foot, as a frail mourning gentlewoman, I could allow for a quarter of an hour. I took my time. Only guilty people hurry, and I did not in any case wish to spend too long outside the chapel before the service began. At the end of the street, I turned the corner and saw a group of people coming in my direction, and for the first time, I was afraid. The full meaning of what I was about spread through me like a sudden fever. I stood for a moment, unable to move. Then I realized, that standing still with no apparent purpose, of loiter-ing, as it were, without intent, was only likely to draw atten-tion to myself, and it was this fear of discovery that propelled my feet forward. It is hard to describe my feelings as I took these next few steps. Perhaps I felt as a child who walks for the first time, with that same mixture of excitement and fear. Of all my clothing, it was the underwear of which I was most conscious. I felt its contours as acutely as if it had been fash-ioned of straw. I stood still again, and looked around for some justification for stopping.

A taxi came in my direction, and for a moment I thought I would hail it for safety. But I was afraid of raising my voice to a volume stronger than mezzo-forte. Since my visit to the 'Femina Boutique', I had undergone a good deal of voice prac-tice, and I had learned my decibel limit, beyond which I would be discovered. My maximum, as I have said, was mezzo-forte, but I was more comfortable and more convincing in the piano range. It was a seductive level, and allowed for a certain auth-entic lowness in pitch, and a shout for a taxi would have been a certain give-away. So I passed the people by, trying to dis-guise my faltering step. But they did not look twice at me, and some of them perhaps not even once, and as I walked along the street, gathering more confidence, passing and being over-taken by more and more people, I noticed that I was the object of no one's attention. On the one hand, this pleased me, but on the other, I was slightly disappointed that no one turned their head to look at me a second time. I felt that my elegant turn-out was worth some acknowledgement.

I had reached the end of the street, and now only had to turn the corner that would lead directly to the crematorium. I could already see the cars as they slowed up to turn into the drive. I felt that if I could make that last hurdle, that entrance into the crowded courtyard outside the chapel, if I could worthily acquit myself in that course, then never again would I return to my old way of life. And it was this desperate ambition which steadied my passage, that carried me unnoticed through the throng, that led me straight past my unknowing wife and up to Mrs Johnson, whose hand I dutifully shook while murmuring my mezzo-forte condolences. And I stood to one side, alone in my beating black, and I knew that, for better or worse, I had committed myself to a course of action that would change my whole existence, and I was filled with such a joy, that for the first time in many years, I thought of my father without pain.

My solitary stance in the courtyard was not conspicuous, for there were many who stood alone in what seemed appropriate contemplation of life and death. Even my wife was holding her tongue, and I moved a little to place myself directly in her line of vision, and she stared right through me without a flicker of recognition. My joy was physical, and I wondered how I had managed for so many years to deprive myself of this quality of fulfilment.

Suddenly an intense quiet struck the gathering, a silence more acute, for it crashed not into a great rumour but into a murmuring. I looked around to see what had prompted this sudden stillness, and I could only ascribe it to the highly conspicuous arrival of the Cloth. Not the Cloth of the Chapel incumbent, but that of my very own, fighting a losing battle to retain what dignity the grand old Parsons had left him. His right eye was covered with a ham-fistedly tied bandage. Its tying had been more a labour of love than technique, and I thought it moist with Miss Price's tears. But despite his appearance, his unstained collar gave him passage, and he strutted through the crowd as if the courtyard were his domain, and that if anybody cramped him, they would be the next for the fire. He managed a condescending smile, for after all, was not every flock his own? Beaten though he was, he looked like a retiring boxer who had made sure of at least half of the purse.

He was making for my wife. That was yet another encounter I had not envisaged, but I cared not what complications would arise from it. Yet my need to eavesdrop urged me to move closer. When he reached my wife, he shattered the silence with what I thought to be an inappropriately loud greeting. 'Afternoon,' he said brusquely. 'Your husband here yet?'

'He won't be coming,' my wife said with a little surprise. 'Pressure of work, he said.'

'He'll turn up all right,' the Cloth said with confidence. 'Gave him permission myself. Ought to be here by now.' He wheeled round to scan the gathering. Did he, or did he not pause for just one second on my frail person? I did not blink, but followed his gaze, and when it returned to my own, I managed with the greatest difficulty to refrain from smiling.

I heard a rustling at my side, and I looked down to see an old lady fumbling in her handbag. I noticed that all around me, bags were being opened in search of props, as a sign that the performance was imminent. In all my purchases, I had forgotten to list a handbag, and I resolved at the next opportunity to remedy this fault. I found myself examining the other women's wear. I already felt one of them, envying a scarf here, a pair of gloves there, offended by a twisted stocking seam, a scuffed pair of shoes. As a man, I had never entertained such thoughts. My indifference to clothing had been sublime. I marvelled that a new dimension of thinking was possible. I had much to look forward to, and I began to wish that they would get on with the business of dispatching my neighbour, to confirm with the fire, his death once and for all, so that I could get on with living.

The Cloth was still scanning the yard for me. 'I wonder what's happened to Verrey Smith,' he said, almost to himself, and at the sound of that name, which over the years had echoed with such noble refrain, I started, for its time-honoured familiarity was suddenly shaken.

'Verrey Smith?' I thought to myself. But its echo, which

hitherto had resolved itself with sure assertion, now hung on the air like an interrupted cadence. I looked down on my clothes, and whatever name they called to mind, it was certainly not Verrey Smith. I felt no sense of betrayal, no treachery to my past. Verrey Smith just did not fit any longer, no more than my trousers and jackets. I wondered what name would become me. I was overcome by a vast sense of freedom that I was able to choose my own identity. It was too important a choice to make casually and I decided to give it more thought, preferably in front of a full-length mirror.

The crowd was moving towards the chapel. I placed myself directly behind the Cloth and my wife, a position that heightened my excitement, and I resolved if possible to sit next to them during the service, in order to prolong my joy, while my neighbour, with bogus testimonial, was launched into the fire. The Cloth gave a last look around the courtyard, probably with thoughts of how to deal with me on the morrow, and I innocently followed his gaze, looking for myself, as well I might, for George Verrey Smith had evaporated. Of that, I was almost sure.

The chapel was small, but large enough to make the gathering look like a sprinkling. All of them seemed to concentrate themselves into two or three rows, close as relations, bound as they were by the common factor of mourning. So it appeared quite natural to seat myself between my wife and my Cloth, and my only problem was to conceal my excitement, a display of which, in this pre-oven climate, would have been most inappropriate. No sooner had we all settled ourselves than, at an unseen prompting, we all rose again, as the coffin was carried through the aisle. I cursed myself for having forgotten a handkerchief, and would have used my glove had I remembered to paint my fingernails. Being a woman was certainly a time-consuming occupation and I resolved in future to put aside a certain hour of my day to my grooming. I put my gloved hand to my eye, wiping away an imagined tear. Even my Cloth was armed with a large white square, which he applied to his bandaged eye, rather pointlessly I thought, since, if there were any mopping-up to be done, that part of his face was well catered

90

for. And so we all dabbed and sighed away, all, that is, except Mrs Johnson whom I could see out of the corner of my eye, silent and imperturbable.

They laid the coffin on the table adjacent to the wall, and it lay there, bare of flowers, an object, cold, dead and beyond anyone's pity. I had never been a promoter of cremation. Death was returnable to the earth, and if there were any hope of an after-life, I saw little point in having oneself chewed up beforehand. One should go to God whole, I thought, to give oneself every chance. There was little dignity in the fire, and an escape from mourning. It was quick and instant disposal that did not allow for the pain of bereavement. For those bereft, I thought, should mourn with ceremony, should devote themselves to keening, should make a cult of it almost. It was the least that the dead deserved. I was trying in my thinking to remain on an abstract level, not daring to particularize, because I knew that, sooner or later, I would think of my father. For he was already flooding my mind. I saw the brutal shovel of earth and my mother's hand trembling. Since he died, I have never been able to weep for him; I have rarely been able to recall him without pain. But now I loved him, and my tears were free. Perhaps it was my clothing that permitted this release. Perhaps I had to reconcile myself with my true identity before I could see him in the role of father. And, but for the location and the hemming-in of my wife and my Cloth, I would have got down on my knees and thanked God for my deliverance. But instead, I wept, and my tears had nothing to do with Mr Johnson. Now the need for a handkerchief, or some kind of wiper, became imperative, and I was bound to take off my glove. Moreover my weeping was aubible, and I heard in its echoes the sobbing that belongs only to childhood. There was nothing I could do to silence it. My wife was looking at me and I trembled that I might be discovered. I was becoming quite central to everyone's attention, and I had thoughts of making a quick get-away. They were whispering behind me, questioning who I was, and I overheard it suggested that the late Mr Johnson had possibly kept a mistress. Their misjudgement flattered me, and gave me great confidence, and I was able to stem the flow a little, and take heed of what their Cloth was about to say about the dear departed. Bent in solemn arc over his desk, he delivered, probably for the hundredth time, his cliché-riddled eulogy that varied only by change of name. Everybody, it seemed, who went through his parish fire, was a good husband/wife/father/mother, revered in his profession/occupation/career, cut down in his prime/ after a good innings, but young or old, doctor or dustman, would most certainly go to God direct from this parish, thereafter let us trust in him, i.e. God/their Cloth, and be comforted. And so they were, as the coffin, on invisible rollers, skated through the hatch and was no more.

I looked at the space it had left behind, an oblong-shaped vacuum, and grief struck me again. The gathering was dispersing, but I remained, and then and there, gazing upon that dreadful vacuum, I buried my own father.

Listen to me. I have tried to tell you before. I really have tried. But now I can tell you. My petticoats permit me. Listen. My father is dead, and it was I who killed him. I as a child, hearing him making a man out of my mother that night of my twelfth birthday. Listen to me. I know I have tried your patience for so long. I have lied, deceived and omitted, but now it's truth I have to tell.

It was that roll of wire. I don't know where it came from or what its purpose was, but it had lain on the shelf in my bedroom for as long as I could remember. Each night it was the last thing I saw before my eyes shut of their own accord, and it coiled my dreams in strangled nightmares. Like any small boy, I longed for amoeba-like dreams without packaging, and that night on my twelfth birthday, I put the roll to some use. I crept out of bed, and tied one end to the bannister support at the top of the stair. The other end I hooked on a spare rail on the opposite side, yet another longstanding object that cried out for function. I surveyed my trap with deep satisfaction, and I crept back into bed. It did not occur to me that my mother would be the first to descend. A child knows with instinctive faith that murder has its own justice. I crouched under the blankets and heard my father's roar. Listen to me,

92

for I must tell it you again, for it is a phrase that has throbbed my heart and that I cannot rinse from my ears. He had done with my mother, I suppose, and as he left the room, he threw it at her. 'Clap yer thighs shut woman. Yer meat stinks.'

I heard their door open, and his clomping step outside. Then almost immediately, the crash. I was afraid to get up, but I heard my mother screaming, and it was for my own protection that I ran to her side.

My father lay on the hall floor, nearly as dead as Mr Johnson, and I hoped desperately, but obviously too late, that my trap had failed. The broken wire dripped on to the staircase, and my mother was staring at it, and then at me, and there was no doubt in her mind as to the connection.

Yes, I killed my father. You have known me long enough. You have been patient with me. You know I am a man who apologizes seldom, and then with great difficulty. Many years ago, *il y a longtemps,* but now there is no need for that, because I am beginning to handle that patricide with my own acknowledged confession. Many years ago, I killed a man. I killed my father, and let my petticoats release my repentance. I am sorry. I am truly sorry.

They all left the little chapel, and I stayed there weeping, in order to bury him for the first time.

As I mourned, I remembered him telling me stories. Even those winter fields I could recall with an understanding that was born of my sudden love. My whole father-studded childhood pounced on me in episodic joy and pain, but all I could peacefully accommodate. I felt like a drowning man who recalls his past, disconnected, parenthetical, but with irrefutable totality. And indeed, I was drowning, for my last image was the frontage of the butcher's shop with the proud name of VERREY SMITH painted and repainted over the generations across the panelled front. And then Verrey Smith died inside me, and I left the chapel, nameless, anonymous, but at peace.

I walked for a long time, up and down streets that I had known for many years. I felt my rambling as a kind of valediction, that I would possibly never tread this route again, I found myself going home, as a last port of call. I went up to my study and packed a small suitcase. Automatically I put in my trousers and jackets, a few shirts and some underwear. I left the clothes and the trimmings my wife had bequeathed me. Though I was not quite myself, whatever that myself was, I still had the cunning to cover my tracks. I intended that George Verrey Smith should disappear, and as far as my wife was concerned, and everybody else for that matter, that he should disappear as a man. For in fact, that was, after all, the true nature of my disappearance. I took what little money I had left, taking care to leave my passport and cheque book conspicuously in evidence on my desk, and crept out of my back door to a new life, I knew not where, how or in what name.

My steps took me towards the school. It was getting dark now, and I had no watch, but as I reached the schoolyard, I saw by the lights in the basement that it was caretaker time. I walked through the playground with faint regrets at the passing of my schoolmastering days, and, as I passed the maintenance shed, I heard a small half-joyful groan. Standing to one side, so that I might not be seen, I had an eyeful of the indomitable Parsons having it off with Washington Jones, one of our quota from the lower third. I turned away, slightly sickened by what I saw, and glad in my heart to be a woman.

I waited at the bus-stop outside the school. I did not fear boarding a bus, and being in close observance of other people. Even the excitement of the con was on the wane. I no longer thought of myself as deceiving anybody. I *was* a woman, in heart and in mind, and deception was no longer a valid proposition.

When the bus arrived, I sat inside. I felt it unladylike to mount the stairs. Such daring would come later, when I ceased to throb under my petticoats. There were few people in the bus and I was able to take a front seat for myself. I looked out of the window, seeing one or two familiar faces, boys from school, shopkeepers and their wives out for the evening. I felt it was illogical to recognize them, for the man who had known them, and acknowledged them each day, was no more. And I

94

knew that there would come a time when my Verrey Smith past would be unrecognizable, so much would I have absorbed my new identity.

And then I saw Miss Price, and I knew that wherever I was, and under whatever guise, the memory of that alarming lady would be with me always. She carried her lonely string shopping bag and clasped a pile of exercise books to that part of her anatomy which in obvious women would be called breast. The conscientious Miss Price always took work home, together with her single lamb chop, and a packet of frozen spinach that was good for her. I watched her probably for the last time and her screaming loneliness pierced me. Yet today perhaps had been one of her happiest, when her Cloth had needed her and she had carried to him, together with the bandages, her sad and stubborn love. I knew I would miss her terribly. Then, as the bus turned the corner and lost her, it suddenly seemed to me right and proper to take upon myself her name. I could do no better than confirm in this way my regard. And so I became Price, with the forename of Emily for sound backing, and the status of widowhood for good measure.

The station was crowded with homegoing commuters. Queues of passengers waited at the ticket booths, or scrambled with their seasons through the barrier. She was pushed and jostled with the rest of them, and with no apology. That was part of the deal too, she thought, and she regretted the lack of gallantry. She waited with patience, and growing inner calm, and as she grew accustomed to her name, rehearsing it in whispers, her voice took on a gentler pitch. Gradually her body was drained of all the anger and the rage that had so lately and for so long held tenancy. She reached the grille, where Emily Price, recently widowed, and in gentle tones, requested a single ticket to Brighton.

Part Two

1

When night fell, with no sign of George, Mrs Verrey Smith decided that the time had come to start worrying. Anxiety would come later, and after that, perhaps sadness. With her great sense of order, one emotion could only be the direct outcome of another. In her feeling patterns, there was no overlap, and she thought that perhaps, whatever happened, she would never reach the sadness stage. Maybe it would all be a great relief. For life with George had not been easy.

Joy Verrey Smith, or Joy Patton, as she had been, had had to come to terms with much in her life. Her mother had died while giving her birth, and her father had never ceased to blame her for it. He had married again, unhappily, and blamed his daughter again for this virago of a second wife. Notwithstanding, he had given her a complete education, and she had trained to be a teacher. She loathed her father, a loathing that was fed by a natural disinclination to her stepmother, but most of all, she disliked herself, and her sole ambition in life was to get married in order to get out of her father's home. It did not occur to her that she could have left home without the drastic step to marriage, but marriage would be an act of self-punishment, and she felt obliged to contribute to the price of her mother's death. This being her only motive, she cared little for the kind of man who would deliver her. Had she been less desperate, she would have examined George Verrey Smith more carefully, but she had rushed him into wedlock not daring to allow herself more time to consider him.

They had met at their amateur dramatic society. Her first part was in a farce. She had played the maid, and George was cast in the role of her mistress's lover. On the sudden unexpected arrival of the husband, George was obliged to change roles with the maid, and to don her clothes. He was desperately unfunny in his part, and during their four nights' run in the local church hall, hardly a titter arose from an audience overwhelmingly related to the cast, and ready to make allowances. But throughout George's cavortings on stage, willing as they were, they could only raise a tired smile, and the only person in the hall who seemed unembarrassed by the proceedings, and indeed, who was positively enjoying them, was George himself. But Joy was willing to overlook all that. It wasn't, after all, as if she wanted to marry an actor. Besides, there were certain qualities George had, difficult to pin-point, she had to admit to herself, but surely there. After the mercifully short run of their first play together, George was never given another part, and he sulked in the wings as assistant stage manager, while any part of a maid that was in the offing went to Joy. And it was probably in this role that George found her most attractive. He too was anxious to free himself from a suffocating mother, and they courted each other, desperately and superficially, and with no questioning on either side, they were married.

The first year had passed uneventfully, though George had displayed certain quirks of behaviour which Joy had thought strange, but which, because of her inexperience, she accepted as part of the marriage pattern. It was normal, she thought, that men could make love to women only if they had corsets on, or perhaps, as in George's case, if they were wearing a corset themselves. Sexual contact was always a nuisance to her anyway, but since it was part of her obligation in the marriage contract, she was prepared to attire herself as George wished. If she had to do it, she was going to do it well and decently, as Joy Verrey Smith did everything else. Joy was a perfectionist except perhaps in her own person. Though her house was spotless, she herself was unclean. She had less respect for skin than for mahogany, and though she would polish with a permanent duster in her hand, spring-cleaning the whole year round, a bath and a change of underwear were for her strictly seasonal. Joy Verrey Smith, née Patton, was an unhappy woman, but

100

this too she had come to terms with, dissipating her energies in lavender polish and laundry. Neighbours who came to tea, which could have been, but wasn't, eaten off the floor, told her that she should start a family. She conveyed their advice to George, who thought it was none of their business. He reminded her that her mother had died when she herself was born, and he suggested that that condition, like madness, was congenital, and he valued her too highly to allow her to run the same risk. She took this information back to her neighbours, who viewed it with suspicion, but suggested in any case, that adoption might be worth consideration. This advice, in its turn, was relayed to George, who reacted quite violently, more at the source of the suggestion, than at the suggestion itself. And so the whole business of children was shelved, and George bought her a pair of budgerigars. Spit and Polish, she called them, and she cleaned and cared for their cage as she might have looked after a pram. Spit and Polish gave Joy Verrey Smith something to live for, something around which her routine could revolve, punctuated twice daily with their feeding. Around about this time, she joined the local women's institute and she took on all kinds of voluntary work. If she would have been a mother, she would have joined the society for the prevention of cruelty to children, but in the budgerigar circumstances, she joined the anti blood-sports and vivisection campaigns. Joy Verrey Smith did nothing by halves. After the acquisition of her birds, her life became one round of meetings, protests and committees, and the odd corseted union with George became an event of seemingly less importance. Though she still accepted his strange little quirks, as she called them, she no longer saw them as normal. Indeed, as she moved more and more in the society of other women, she began to suspect something very perverse about her husband, and it was through the birds that her suspicions were finally confirmed.

It was her habit to buy a week's supply of birdseed and feed them regularly twice a day. Yet sometimes, by midweek, her stock had run out, and she considered whether George was feeding them too. He denied it, but she caught a strange flush over his face. Her seed-stock depleted itself more and more often over the next weeks and though she looked everywhere, she could not account for its disappearance. Until one Monday morning. George had gone to school, and Joy loaded the week's wash into her wheeler shopping cart to take to the launderette. Mrs Bakewell was already there, and most of the neighbours. Monday morning at the launderette was a social event for Joy Verrey Smith. She had come to know the women intimately, and not only the women but their families too. Although she had only a nodding acquaintance with Mr Bakewell, she knew his underwear intimately. So much so, that it had become embarrassing to acknowledge him, wondering whether he knew that she knew that his underpants were cotton-flowered, and his vest, whichever one he had on, was torn. The women seemed to have no shame in displaying what was after all a very private affair, and in an unlaundered state at that. For herself, she did not want to be wholly known, and she would turn away to shake out the underwear before loading it into the machine. And on that Monday morning as she turned about to shake out their smalls, a great shower of budgerigar seed scattered all over the launderette floor, and on investigation, she found that it had come from the two cups of her white brassière. She turned around and looked at the others with a sheepish grin. 'Heaven knows how that got there,' she said feebly, knowing full well how, and more terribly, why. But she would deal with that later. Her neighbours would have to be pacified first. 'I've been looking for that seed all week,' she tried manfully. 'Must have dropped it into the laundry basket.' It didn't sound very feasible, but it would have to do. She finished loading the wash, trying to make her mind an absolute blank, and when it was done, she excused herself from the others, saying she wanted to do some quick shopping. She positively fled out of the launderette and found a café nearby. Hiding herself in a corner, her hands clasping a cup of froth she didn't want, she told herself it was time to think about what had happened. But try as she would, there was no alternative explanation of the presence of birdseed in her bra. He – my God, what kind of man had she married? – he had worn it. Of that there was no question. And he had stuffed the cups for authenticity. How long had it been going on? And what in heaven's name had he been wearing on top of the bra, and did he go out in it, and what kind of man...? Suddenly the corseted unions became clear to her, and certain of his habits, his liking for darning, or polishing, or even, occasionally baking a cake. She didn't know what these sort of men were called, but she knew instinctively that they weren't normal. She was not moved by it; she simply had no patience with it. Whatever it was called in those fancy books by psychiatrists, it was dirty and rude, and she was enraged at the possibility of her poor little budgies going hungry in such a filthy cause. She decided that she would tackle him as soon as he came home. She would have liked to have been able to go into his study to ferret out more evidence of his filth. But it was locked and double-locked, always, possibly in fear of that very intrusion. However, she had enough to go on with to confront him and perhaps more would emerge in the cross-examination.

All day she did nothing but wait for him to come home, rehearsing the questions with her birds, polishing their cage all the while to give vent to her rage and indignation. 'You sure you haven't seen the birdseed?' she shouted at Spit and Polish. Then, after a pause, 'Then maybe, you've seen my white bra?' She repeated these questions endlessly, and it was on the first of these, asked of the birds for the hundredth time, that George surprised her, coming through the back door into the kitchen. She turned around, the question still hanging, and he made as if to back away, his face a pale green, and trembling with what seemed to him to be a total discovery.

'What are you talking about?' he said, playing for time, but knowing that in the end there was no escape. In fact, he experienced a faint sense of relief that she had come to know about it. All he could hope for was her anger, and noncomprehension. If she were to sympathize with him, or worse, to understand him, it would be unbearable. And so he did not bother to defend himself. His attitude was that it was, after all, his own business, and he could choose to dress as he pleased.

'Yes,' she screamed at him, 'but not in my clothes.'

'Then I shall get them elsewhere.'

'In a shop?' she said, horrified.

'There are women's clothes in other women's wardrobes,' he said quietly. He started to fill the kettle as if, on his side, the conversation was at an end.

'There are corsets too,' she said. 'But I've discovered it's not natural to wear them in bed. You've made a freak out of me, too. Well, I hope you can find another.'

'That won't be difficult,' he said, 'and it's not that I haven't thought of trying.'

He hadn't meant to go that far. He had never thought of looking elsewhere. His wife was adequate to his needs, and in any case, the whole notion of adultery offended him. He wished he had not threatened her. But his wife had left the room and it was too late for apology, something he never in any case indulged in. As far as he was concerned, he was rarely wrong, and never, never sorry. So he got on with the tea-making, and by the time the table was set, she had returned. She looked as if she had been crying, but the rage had not left her. She sat primly at her end of the table. 'I don't want to discuss it any more,' she said, meaning that she was going to have her own say, but that she had no intention of listening to him. 'I find the whole business disgusting and, until you mend your ways, you will sleep in your study. I am going to lock my bedroom door.'

Which she did. Over the weeks, he made occasional attempts to get in, never knocking, never pleading, but aggressively demanding his rights. Perhaps, had he begged her, apologized for his misguided ways, had he made her feel the victim and ultimately, the forgiving one, perhaps she would have relented. But his aggression only served to cement her will, though she rarely used foul language, she cursed him through the door, as his sense of being wronged became more acute.

And then, after a few weeks, he stopped coming to her door altogether, and she would hear him go out at night and come home very early in the morning. She knew that he had carried out his threat, and she began to regret her hastiness. She had been almost sure that he would not be able to find another woman who could cater to his perversities. She was not to know that parts of London were full of them, and probably offering a great deal more than he had fantasized in his wildest dreams. And in fact, this is exactly what George had done. He had found a regular, Mavis, a good many years older than himself, but who was more than willing. At first, he enjoyed her, the anonymity of the situation excited him. But gradually Mavis palled. It was not her ageing body. On the contrary, when corseted, age was far more attractive to George than youth. But he missed his wife, for his wife had found nothing unnatural in his mode of congress. She had accepted it as if it were naturally expected from her. But Mavis, though willing, found the whole procedure disgusting, and never ceased to cheapen it, and that made George find it disgusting too. But he could not bring himself to equate perversity with his own person, and in the end, after only a few weeks, he had to leave her, expelled by Mavis's own contempt.

By the time he came back, Joy was more than ready to receive him, but she kept her door locked as before. She still wanted his apology, and in those early days of her marriage, she hadn't fully understood that her husband was incapable of contrition. But she hoped, nonetheless, and one day she thought of a way of reopening negotiations, without it appearing that she was doing the asking. So at supper one evening, she asked him if he had any old clothes to give to the church jumble sale. She herself was sorting out her wardrobe, she told him. She waited, hoping for some reaction. But he was a man who would never ask anyone for anything, because to no one would he be beholden. He was in all senses a mean man, and for a moment, she hated him. But she had married him, and it was the status of marriage that she was above all holding on to. 'I'm sorting out my wardrobe,' she said again. 'There are so many things I'm tired of. They're still in very good condition.' She tried to conceal the pleading in her voice. 'It seems a pity to be giving them away.'

'Then don't,' he said, 'but if you're not wearing them, there's no point in them hanging there, is there?'

'Then what shall I do with them?' she tried again.

'Why ask me?' he said. 'Give them away. I'll sort mine out too.' He was not going to give her an opening so that she could give him one too. He knew well what she wanted to offer, that she wanted to come together again with him, but she bloody well would have to ask, to beg, for it was she who had locked the door in the first place.

'Some are too good to give away,' she said almost tearfully. She looked at him and felt a bitter hatred in her heart. 'Would you like them?' she almost shouted at him.

'D'you realize what you're offering?' he said with a sneer. 'In the name of whose so-called perversion have you locked your bedroom door? Yours or mine?' He was going to make her offer him her clothes on her bended knees. And he wanted everything too, underwear, jewellery accessories, yes, and bras as well, and as much birdseed to cater for the day's fashion.

'I'll give them away then. Perhaps you have changed your little habits.'

He had goaded her too far. He wanted her clothes, badly. Especially the black ones, and that blue chiffon that he knew she was tired of. 'Don't give them away if they're too good,' he said. 'You should sell them.'

'What are you offering?' she said.

He didn't answer, knowing that her capitulation was only a matter of time.

'I'll give them to you,' she said in despair. She got up quickly from the table and went to her room. She had already laid the clothes out on her bed, her black indispensable, her blue chiffon and sundry accessories. She took the dresses and crumpled them furiously, wringing them out as if wet. At least he'd have to go to the trouble of ironing them. She rolled all the clothes together, tying up the bundle with a torn petticoat, and threw the lot outside his study door. As she went downstairs, he crossed her silently on the staircase. He went into his study and he stayed there for a long time. That night, she left their bedroom door unlocked, and once again, they renewed their corseted congress.

So after all those joyless years, those childless, corseted,

106

budgerigar years, perhaps it would be a relief if George had disappeared for ever. But at such a thought, she grieved a little, for over the years she had come to understand him, had reluctantly at first, and then willingly, played the victim for his sake. He had to come back for the sake of the battle. Moreover, she was stunned by their years together. Seventeen years. She could not envisage a Georgeless life, either now, or before her marriage. It would be easier if he were dead, like Mr Johnson. At least Mrs Johnson knew where she stood. But relief or no, grief or no, it was midnight, and time to start worrying. He could, of course, have started an outside fling again, but there had been no warnings of that. On the contrary, of late, their marriage, though silent and occasionally spiteful, had been a successful connection, in fact, more so than in the early days. He had seemed fraught occasionally, but that was probably due to pressure of school work. Occasionally, he had even been happy. She could not imagine that there was someone else, though in a way she would have preferred it, because she could cope with anger more efficiently than with anxiety. It had not occurred to her to go to his study to look for extra clues to his disappearance. That room would be locked, and double locked, as always. So she decided to go to bed and wait for him, expecting him in the early hours, giving her time to rehearse a tirade. She fed her birds from her own stock – she had even consented to buy George seed for his own use. Now she bitterly resented that concession. She covered their cage and went upstairs. On the landing, she stopped. Not only was the study door unlocked, not only was it ajar, but it was flung open as if inviting entry. And when she saw that abandoned stronghold, she knew that he had retreated from battle, and that she was alone on the mangled pitch. She hesitated to go inside. She had never been in the room alone. When she cleaned it, it was always under his supervision, and he would follow her around, allowing her to touch only surfaces and forbidding her to open drawers or cupboards. So she was frightened to go in alone, dreading what the room would have to offer. Automatically she looked around to see if she were being spied on. Entrance to that room alone had been so strictly forbidden that she could not trust that she wasn't being put to some kind of test. She went slowly to the study and peered about, fearing that he might be inside and waiting for her. But the room was empty, and moreover the wardrobe door hung open, and the drawers of his desk were ajar. She touched nothing. Her conditioning had been so acute, she was afraid to move without supervision. In the wardrobe she could see his collection of Sunday clothes, that over the years she had given him. But all his own clothes, his suits, shirts and jackets were gone, all except his old school blazer which he had never worn but kept for old times' sake. On the desk lay his passport and cheque book. Her desperation gave her courage and she looked through his drawers and his desk-papers, but found no letter, no address, no clue whatsoever to his disappearance. But she had a feeling he had gone for ever. He had given up the Sunday life, he had left as a man, without possessions, and she was forced to conclude that he must have gone to a monastery. But the disappearance of all his clothes scotched that possibility. He could, of course, have drawn another cheque book and left that one on the desk as a red herring. But that could easily be checked with the bank. She really didn't know how to start tracking him down or whether she should start at all. She looked in the bathroom for any evidence he might have left behind. His razor was gone, and that with George was significant. He shaved rarely, possibly only once a week. She had often admired his almost womanish lack of hair. Now she understood. If his razor was gone, he intended to go on living and once again she tried to convince herself that he would be back by morning. She went to bed, leaving the door open, and all the lights on, for the lights sharpened her hearing, and she would know the moment he returned.

She woke early next morning, with the door still open and the light still on, and George patently not there. She went into his study again thinking perhaps that he had sneaked in during the night and left a note, but it was as she had left it. She decided to let the morning pass. If he weren't at school, the headmaster would phone, and then she would know that he had really disappeared. His absence from school would close up all other loopholes, and she would have to go to the police. She fed Spit and Polish without her customary affection. She missed setting the table for his breakfast, hurrying over her own so that she could serve him. From force of habit, she ate quickly, and then was faced with the morning, still early, with little incentive to do anything, even to clean the already spotless house, an activity never once foregone in all her married life. She wanted to tell somebody but she didn't know as yet what there was to be told. She felt she ought to be frantic, she felt she ought at least to be crying, but there was a numbness about her, fed perhaps by the hope that he would come back, and his night out held some valid explanation. But she recalled the open study door and experienced a fleeting moment of panic. It was still only 8.30. She couldn't expect a phone call from the school for at least an hour. They would allow a little time for his being late. She dreaded that the phone would ring and confirm his disappearance, and she toyed with the idea of going to the Rotary committee meeting that had been called for 10.30. She could go out early, now even, and miss the phone call if it ever came. But she decided that she would have to wait for him. For his confirmed absence or presence she would have to be there.

The phone rang at 9.30. She hesitated before answering. But it could be George, she thought, so she picked up the phone with less fear. It was the Reverend Richard Baines himself.

'Mrs Verrey Smith? Headmaster here. Your husband not well, this morning?'

'No. No,' she stammered. She had received the information. She was not obliged to tell him that George had disappeared. 'He's not well,' she said. ' 'Flu, I think,' with feeble invention. 'That's why he wasn't at the funeral. Found him in bed when I got home. The doctor came last night and said it would take a few days. I was going to ring you later, but I'm waiting for the doctor.' She was becoming obsessively chatty and the Cloth was anxious to get a word in.

'I'm sorry,' he said, with a complete absence of regret. 'Makes me very short-handed. Seemed all right to me yesterday morning. Nevertheless, wish him well. I may call to see him. Part of my extra-mural duties, you know.' He put the phone down before she had time to wonder how to put him off. She regretted her dishonesty. It only complicated matters for her. But there was still a whole day in which he could make a sudden reappearance, and she had to stay at home, both for that, and for the headmaster's promised visit, when ever that would be. But she had to tell somebody. Having decided on Mrs Bakewell as her confidante, she knew not what to tell her. If George did come home, it would be a pity if anyone had known of his disappearance. So she had to hold her tongue. She went to the window, and looked hopefully down the street but, save for the laundryman, it was empty. Absentmindedly, she fed the birds again. Spit and Polish, confused by their good fortune, fought over the second helping, and she covered the cage to punish them. She sat down again at the table. She had not cleared the breakfast dishes. She half made a decision never to clean the house again until George returned. She realized what a complete and radical difference this would make to her life, a life punctuated by polish and elbow-grease. But now she needed all her energies to cope with George's disappearance. He had to come back or the house would go to rack and ruin. She lit a cigarette. She smoked very rarely, not wanting to dirty the ashtrays. But that life was already behind her. She would chain-smoke until George returned. As she lit her cigarette, the phone rang. That was George. It had to be. He'd been held up somewhere, lost his memory or something, any feeble excuse she was more than ready to accept. She ran to the telephone.

'Mrs Verrey Smith?'

It was the headmaster again. She was terrified. Did he have information she knew nothing of?

'Mrs Verrey Smith?' he said again. 'The most terrible thing has happened.'

'Oh my God,' she said, 'has anything happened to George?'

'George?' he said. 'How should I know, my good woman, if

anything has happened to your husband? He's in bed at home, isn't he, or so you said.'

'I'm sorry, headmaster, I'm just a little confused. I'm worried about George, that's all. I'm running up and down the stairs all the time. He's not a good patient as you can imagine. I'm a little confused, that's all.' She knew she had to stop being chatty. It was the chat that liars used as cover, and the headmaster, thick as he was, was bound to see through it.

'Anyway,' he said, 'I'm sorry about that, but I've got to talk to him.' She hesitated. 'He's sleeping at the moment,' was all she could say, wondering how this fact could tally with all the running up and down stairs she was doing after him. 'I'd rather not wake him. But I could give him a message,' she said, willing to help, 'and he could ring you back.'

'Well, it's confidential of course, but I can tell you, since you're his wife, and it is a matter in which he is most urgently concerned. The most dreadful thing has happened. I have just been informed that Mr Parsons – you heard about the Parsons affair, I suppose – but that's of no consequence at the moment, well I've just been informed that poor Mr Parsons's body has been found behind the maintenance shed. He was found there early this morning, murdered. Now the police are investigating of course – a terrible interruption of the curriculum – and they are bound to interview all members of the staff. Now I'm not for one moment suggesting that your husband has anything to do with the matter. In fact it seems he has a better alibi than most of us. Ha ha. At least his doctor, who as you said visited him last night, can confirm his whereabouts for the police seem to think that Parsons had been dead for at least twelve hours. But the police must see him. If he is not well enough to come to the school, then the police will insist on coming to the house. This is a dreadful business,' he went on, 'and I'm sorry to upset you, but if it will help, I'll come along with the police to soothe matters.'

'Yes, do,' she said, as if she were inviting him for a cup of tea. 'I'm sure George will help all he can.'

She replaced the receiver, because the Cloth had rung off, and she sat at the table, no longer considering George as an adulterer, nor even as a monk manqué, seeking refuge in a monastery, but as a murderer, and she shuddered at the terrible implications for both him and for herself, and how this sudden unaccountable disappearance would single him out as the prime suspect. 'George,' she screamed into the lonely empty house, 'for God's sake, come home, get into bed, have 'flu, be ill, be dying, honestly and decently in your bed, anything, anything but a murderer.' She had never known Parsons and had no idea of what the headmaster had meant by the Parsons affair. If only she could find out, it might shed some light on George's disappearance. But whom could she ask? Whom could she tell? There was little point now in going to the police. They would be here soon enough on other matters, and then it would all be out under an open dark cloud.

She went over to the window again, and stared out into the empty street. She saw the Johnson door open, and she wondered who could be taking the air from that house of mourning. It was Tommy, and he seemed to steal out of the house looking back at the front door to make sure he was not seen. He crept down the side of the path, brushing his legs against the low privet hedge, and once out of the gate, he made a dive for the Verrey Smith front door, bounding up the path, knocking loudly for immediate entry. She knew that he must have news of George. Tommy never came to call on her. As his form teacher's wife, she was strictly out of visiting bounds. And his news was urgent too. He had left a house of mourning to tell it. It had to be about George.

And indeed it was. He stood panting at the door. 'Mrs Verrey Smith,' he said. 'Your 'usband's my Dad. My Mum told me.'

He was gone before she could digest his news. As she closed the door, the impact of this new piece of information prickled her flesh. It could not be a joke. The boy was in no mood to be funny. He had been desperately serious. That was clear. So George had kept her childless for seventeen years, and had gone next door to sire. But she did not hate him for it. It was Mrs Johnson she hated, and now she understood why her neighbours had shed no tears at the funeral. But George had

112

gone. He had left her, and presumably also a son, and – she dared not think of it – perhaps he had left behind a corpse as well. She went into the kitchen, and leaning against the door, she sobbed aloud. 'Come home, George. For God's sake, come home.'

2

When Emily Price, recently widowed, alighted from the train at Brighton station, she put down her suitcase and wondered what to do. Throughout the hour or so journey from London, she had been too intent on being Emily Price to give much thought as to what Emily Price was going to do on arrival. People passed her by, rushing along the platform, anxious to get home, to suppers, to television sets, to recaps of the day, and in spite of her new identity which should have been company enough, Emily Price had a sinking feeling of loneliness. A young man, passing by in less of a hurry than the others, stopped by her side. 'Can I help you?' he said. 'You seem very lost.'

She hesitated before speaking. Not since her change only a few hours ago, though it seemed a lifetime, had she been directly encountered in speech. She trembled and the man took it for shyness and placed his hand on her arm. Thus encouraged, she whispered, 'Do you know of a quiet hotel? I've nowhere to stay.'

He smiled at her, and she wondered how he saw her. Like his own mother perhaps, a trifle younger, but not young enough, she prayed to God, to warrant any more than his gentlemanly attentions. Although such an eventuality had occurred to her on viewing older men on the train, a possibility both exciting and frightening, she was not prepared to deal with it so soon. She gave him back a smile, a motherly one she hoped, and he took her arm as if he would look after her. Yes, he did know of a small hotel and he would take her there. His car was outside the station. He always left it there in the morning when he came up on the London train. He was in insurance, he told her without being asked. She was in any case, still too unsure of her speech to invite any dialogue. She wondered at his forthcoming manner, and whether he was like this with everyone. She hoped that he wasn't that lonely that he would have to pick up friendships on station platforms. Yet there was something quite desperate about him for one so young, a need to be totally known by a perfect stranger. They had reached the car by the time he'd touched the subject of his family. His father had died of a thrombosis three years ago, though he assured her that a heart condition was not conspicuous in his family tree. His mother lived alone in a little house on the Hove end, but he himself had moved into a small flat nearer the station. Yes, she was a wonderful woman, his mother, a little eccentric, you know, leaning over the passenger seat and locking the door from the inside. His mother had her little quirks, but then, women alone, he generalized, often fell into odd little habits. Emily was curious as to what form these strange habits took, and she hoped that with this subject, as with all others, he would elaborate. But he left them as 'quirks' and nothing more, and it was clear that he did not want to go into them. He turned the car into a main shopping street, firing a direct question on the turn.

'Have you got a job in Brighton?'

'No, not yet,' she said slowly and quietly. 'I shall be looking for one.'

'D'you do any special kind of work?'

'I thought I'd look for a job as a lady's companion. That would solve my accommodation problem as well.' She gave a deep sigh. She had uttered a long, long sentence, her first serious communication as a woman, and he was totally convinced by her.

'You must meet my mother,' he said. 'She often talks of having someone to live with her. The house is so big and she gets a bit lonely.' He had turned into a side street and pulled up outside a tall Victorian house in a terraced row. An 'Apartments to Let' sign hung in the front window. From the look of the house, the young man had understood Emily's pocket, and

115

she was grateful to him. Without thinking she put a hand on his arm and thanked him.

The young man seemed to know the hotel owner, and Emily was settled in with no difficulty. He carried her bag to the door, and took out his card and wrote his mother's name and telephone number on the back. 'I'll tell her about you,' he said. 'Please get in touch. You never know. You might be happy to stay with her.' He shrugged his shoulders as if this were a very doubtful possibility. She thanked him again.

'You have been very kind,' she said. 'I hope it's not been too much out of your way.' She patted his cheek to confirm the generation gap, but she realized her mistake, as he in turn, patted hers. In panic, she wondered whether he felt the stubble, and she felt herself blushing. He smiled at what he took to be her shyness. 'I'll see you again,' he said. 'I'm sure of that.'

Emily went to her room and straight to the dressing-table mirror. No stubble was visible and she felt her cheek. It was possible that he hadn't noticed. She hadn't shaved for four days. In her old life, once a week had always been her shaving pattern. So little hair grew, that even that sometimes was not necessary, and she was grateful for her hairlessness now.

She sat on the bed and examined the room. The dressing-table top delighted her. It held many glass bowls and jars, and one bowl even held a powder puff. It was very much a woman's room, with lace and chintz curtains, and a flowered candlewick bedspread. On the bedside table was a small lamp with a crocheted cover with a cluster of china roses as its base. She put her case on the bed, and on opening it, remembered she had nothing to change into. Neither could she unpack. A wardrobe of men's clothing would betray her to the proprietor. She dared not wash her face, for she had no make-up replacement. She counted out her money. There was enough for a week's stay at the hotel together with food, and the bare essentials of make-up. She would have meantime to find a post and accommodation. She closed her case again and put it under the bed. She would have to get a job pretty soon in order to ac-

116

cumulate enough money to buy the essentials to prolong her deception.

She decided to take a walk along the promenade, with perhaps a cup of tea somewhere, before retiring. She locked the door and took the key. Outside she crossed over the main road and leaned over the barrier to look at the sea. The enormity of the change that had taken place in her, and the complicated machinations of that change, suddenly depressed her. For a moment she thought of returning to the hotel, to her trousers and jacket in the suitcase, and of going back to London. But having tasted the joys of being a woman, she was loathe now to go back to a life of fiction. She thought of her wife with remorse. It was a sensation that was totally new to her and opened up possibilities of a wider pattern of feeling than she had ever known before. It was frightening. Her new commitment needed more courage than her old. It was the lack of money and the solitude of it all, she told herself. She felt a tear on her cheek and shivered at a sudden unaccountable thought of her mother. She had surrendered her old life and the greatest compensation of that surrender was the destruction of its eternal travelling companion, her father. Had she wrought such a change in herself, only to pick up yet another familiar one even more unaccommodating than the last? It did not bear thinking about. She looked back at the sea, and its enormity and its faint suggestions of God and eternity had a depressing effect on her. She went back to her hotel and ordered tea in her room.

She wanted very much to cry but, mindful of her purse, crying was impractical. She needed to hold on to her make-up until replacement was available. And so she cried inside herself. It would be easy to go home, she thought. Joy would be lost without her, and the boys in her class; they would miss her too, she hoped. She could still get the late train back to London, and change into George in the lavatory. She would think up some excuse for the evening's absence. But in the end, the thought sickened her. The name of George Verrey Smith was not yet alien enough to unruffle her, and when she recalled it, it was with nausea. No, a going back was now impossible. She had buried her father once and for all, and that burial had given her birth. And now she could not stem the tears, knowing that she could never go home again, because Emily Price had overtaken her.

3

It was five o'clock in the evening, and Joy Verrey Smith had not seen her husband for thirty-two hours. During the day she had smoked endlessly, and drunk tea, moving between the kitchen table and the net curtains in the front room. Now she sat down, shrivelled in anguish, recapping the terrifying items of information that had punctured her day. Her husband had disappeared. Mr Parsons had been murdered. Tommy next door was her stepson. She tried to think of each item separately, because in her heart she refused them any connection. She did not think of what she would tell the police when they came, as come they must, sooner or later. But she knew what she would not tell them. There would be no mention of Tommy, nor of George's little hobby. That much respect she had for him, and, now as the hours of his absence lengthened, that much love.

She got up again to go to the curtain, and as she crossed the hall the bell rang. Through the frosted window pane, she could discern the Cloth's unbroken collar. He was alone. There were no shadows around him. She would have to tell him the truth. George had simply disappeared and he could infer what he liked from it. She opened the door.

'Good evening, Mrs Verrey Smith,' he said. 'I've told the police to come through the back entrance. Thought it might embarrass you if the whole street were to see their arrival. They're in uniform, you know.'

'That's thoughtful of you,' she said, asking him in, though she resented the criminal aura he'd shed on the visit. When they reached the front room they heard the police tapping on the kitchen door. Four of them, looking as if they had come to make an arrest. They all settled in the kitchen.

'May we go up?' the Cloth said. 'Just a few questions. Horrible business, Mrs Verrey Smith, but the Force have to question everybody.' His tone was deferential, strictly on the side of the Law. Only of God would he speak with greater respect.

She sat down on the kitchen chair, and they wondered why she was holding up proceedings. 'He's not here,' she said simply. 'I haven't seen him since he left for school yesterday morning.'

The posse rocked in one movement drawing the more than obvious conclusion. The Cloth sat down heavily and salivated. 'But Mrs Verrey Smith,' he stammered, 'you said he had the 'flu. You brought us here to see him. How most misleading of you.' He looked at the Force with abject apology. He was going to be on the right side of the Law whoever was chairman.

'I didn't know how to tell you,' she said helplessly. 'I hoped he'd come back during the day.'

It seemed there was no special spokesman for the Force, and though all four minds flooded with the identical thought, not one of them wished to voice it.

'Well, come now,' said the Cloth, as detective manqué, 'there seems to be some inference here. Mr Parsons is found murdered, and Mr Verrey Smith has disappeared.' He spelt it out loud and clear as if from the pulpit. 'I think perhaps some questions are in order.' He had given them their cue and they looked at each other offering one another the floor.

'I think we need the Superintendent for this one,' the most courageous of them offered. 'May I use your phone, Madam?'

He went into the hall, and though there was absolute silence in the kitchen, and ears on all sides were strained, it was difficult to decipher the conversation. After a while he came back, and announced that the Superintendent was on his way, and they rocked sideways together, as if barring her exit should she have her escape in mind. No word was said between them, and even Spit and Polish, who normally at this hour sang their little throats out, cowered with an instinctive recognition of the uniform, both of the Law and of the Cloth. They both turned their backs on the gathering and nestled close to each other. Again Mrs Verrey Smith recapped her items of information but, even at this stage and in the tangible presence of the police, she refused to connect them. She had to break the silence with some kind of protest. If she said nothing, it could be deduced that she agreed with their obvious conclusions. She addressed herself to the Cloth. 'I refuse to see any connection between my husband's disappearance and the death of Mr Parsons. I don't honestly see why one has anything to do with the other.' She was getting angry now. 'I think it most premature of you to make any such suggestion.' She hated the Cloth, and now she understood why George had hated him too, and again she felt a stab of love for her vanished husband.

'We shall see,' the Cloth said, and she was sure she saw him smile. She turned her back on him. She would not entertain him with her tears.

They sat for a long time in silence, and she wished the Superintendent would arrive. The phone rang as they waited and, as she got up to answer it, the Cloth restrained her. 'Perhaps we'd better leave it to the police,' he suggested. He nodded in their direction and, on command as it were, one of them crossed into the hall. The Cloth was having a whale of a time, and could hardly bear to wait to hear who it was. The policeman returned.

'It's a Mrs Bakewell for you, Madam,' he said. 'She'd like to talk to you.'

She got up. 'I see no reason for you to answer my phone,' she said. As her husband's case appeared to her to be more and more shaky, she became aggressive and resentful. 'You are treating me as if I were a criminal,' she said. 'You too,' she nodded at the Cloth hoping that, if George ever came back, he would never want to return to that school. She went into the hall and picked up the receiver. Mrs Bakewell was avid to know who had answered the phone, and seemed less than satisfied when Mrs Verrey Smith told her it was the electrician who was expecting a call from his firm. She did not feel like talking to Mrs Bakewell, who in any case had only rung up for a chat, as was her wont, this time of the evening. She was anxious to get back to the kitchen, in case the conspirators were talking about her. She hoped the Superintendent would come soon. Anything was better than their continued accusing silence.

When he arrived, in a large police car, and by the front door, it was with an air of authority and ability to take absolute control. 'This is a police matter,' he said to the assembled company on arrival, and his opinion could only have been meant for the Cloth, who was neither witness nor prosecutor.

'I thought perhaps I might stay by Mrs Verrey Smith's side,' he said. 'Rather upsetting business for her, a woman alone, I would think.'

Yes, it was indeed, Joy thought, but the Cloth in the role of consort would help little and she was glad when the Superintendent assured him that he would not be needed. In fact, he started to propel him towards the front door. The Cloth's collar did not impress him. He had a job to do, and no doubt the Cloth likewise, and they had both better get on with it.

'I'll come to see you tomorrow,' the Reverend Richard Baines threw from the front door. He had to be kept informed. Mr Verrey Smith was, after all, one of his staff, he explained to the Superintendent, and his welfare was part of his concern. The Superintendent shut the door on him and returned to the kitchen. He told his men to wait in the hall while he talked to the lady.

Now they were gone, and he looked as if he were determined to wring every item of information out of her, while she, staring back at him, was equally determined to withold at least part of it. There was still a chance that George would come back, and the less known of him the better.

The Superintendent took out his notebook, and began with routine questioning. She told him what he already knew, that her husband had disappeared, and that she could find no reason to account for it. No, he had no financial problems, no other woman, no phase of deep depression. 'My husband is perfectly normal,' she challenged him and it was her aggression that aroused his suspicions.

'I hate to ask you these personal questions, Mrs Verrey Smith, but it is in all our interests that your husband be found.

He may have absolutely nothing to do with the murder. His disappearance may be purely coincidental. But you agree, that until we find him, we cannot clear him. Are you sure there was no other woman?'

It suddenly occurred to Mrs Verrey Smith that George might be hiding next door, but she kept this idea to herself. 'My husband and I have been married for seventeen years. We have always been happy together. As far as I know, he has never been with another woman.' The misery of their years together was no business of the Superintendent. A man who could commit murder could commit other things too, and she had to prove George guilty of nothing. For a moment she considered whether it was remotely possible that George had had a hand in Mr Parsons's undoing, but she dismissed the thought. It would have been a victory for the Superintendent if he had managed to plant such a thought in her mind.

'I would like to search the house,' he said suddenly.

'But why?' she said. 'He's not here. You don't think I'm hiding him?'

'Not for one moment, Mrs Verrey Smith, but there may be some clues as to his disappearance, or even, though I doubt it, some evidence of a connection with the late Mr Parsons. I'm afraid I have a warrant,' he said, seeing the beginning of her protest. 'It would be of help to yourself, I'm sure, if you would be of help to me. Does your husband have his own room? A study, perhaps? I presume you share a bedroom.'

'Yes,' she said, leading the way. 'I'll take you to his study.'

In the hall, the Superintendent motioned the men to follow. On the stairs she explained to him how he always kept the study door locked, and how, on returning home after the funeral, she had found it open. That was all he needed to know, she thought, and suddenly remembered his sundays, hanging in his closet. One of the policemen had already opened the wardrobe door, and she was beside him with overflowing explanation. 'They're mine, those clothes,' she said. 'I'm sorting out my things to give to a jumble sale. I hung them in there for the time being. It's in aid of handicapped children you know. We have one every year.' She heard her endless chat as from an unsure liar. 'Anyway,' she ended, 'they're mine.' Then she wondered why she'd made an issue of them at all. They were palpably hers, wherever they were hanging, and her vociferousness had not been lost on the Superintendent. He called her aside.

'For everyone's sake,' he said, 'it would be better if you confided in me. You have told me that your husband always kept this door locked. There is a divan in this room. There are also women's clothes in the cupboard. Is it not possible that your husband was keeping another woman, and that you, rather than lose him completely, decided to turn a blind eye?' He was giving her a very convenient get-out, and it was certainly preferable to be married to an adulterer rather than a murderer. She decided to fall into the net. It would give George a reason for his disappearance, and would also help to remove the suspicion that was tailing him.

'Yes,' she said. 'He did occasionally have other women, and I think lately, he had someone quite regularly. But I don't know who she was. But the clothes are mine, that's true.' She didn't want them taking them away and finally discovering that they belonged to her. 'I'm having a sort out of my clothes. I'm putting the overflow in here. My husband always kept his clothes in his study. Our bedroom closet is too small. I'll show it to you,' she said, chattily again. She was now willing to give him every ounce of collaboration, any story that would detract suspicion from George, even if it reflected poorly on herself. For a moment she hated her husband, and wondered whether he was worth even the slightest stain on her own reputation. She began to wonder whether there were indeed other women, others apart from Mrs Johnson. But it would be useless to ask her. She intended to ignore Tommy's declaration. As far as she was concerned, Tommy was an orphan. But at this thought, she saw George dead, murdered in a back alley, and she shuddered. Her mind was so confused. She wanted to love George, she wanted him back, but her mind kept getting in the way.

'We must have a photograph of him,' the Superintendent was saying. 'We must circularize his details.'

'I haven't got a photograph,' she said quickly.

One of the policemen picked up the passport from the desk. 'Here's one,' he said, opening it. 'Quite recent, too.' He handed the document to the Superintendent who put it in his pocket.

'D'you have a full-length photograph?' he said, ignoring her last remark.

'Only a wedding one, and that was seventeen years ago. He's changed a lot since then.'

'What was he wearing when he left?'

Again she was loath to give information. She did not want George found until Parsons's murderer had confessed. Then his way back would be clear.

'Was he wearing a suit perhaps?' The Superintendent tried to help her.

'No,' she said. A suit was more findable than a nondescript pair of trousers and jacket. 'He had grey trousers on, I think, and a small checked jacket. I don't recall what shirt or tie.' That was true. She rarely noticed George for he himself gave no attention to it either. She had given the Superintendent very little to go on with, and he took the passport out of his pocket. 'Was your husband clean-shaven? I mean, did he, when he left, have either a moustache or a beard?'

She shook her head. She could not imagine George bearded.

'How long would it take your husband to grow a moustache, would you think? Does his hair grow very quickly?'

'Oh yes,' she lied. 'He could have the beginnings of a fine beard in a week.'

The Superintendent looked at the photograph again. 'He seems to have a very fair skin,' he said. 'I wouldn't have thought him a hairy man myself.' He made a note. He clearly did not believe her. 'How tall is your husband?' he went on.

'Six foot,' she said, giving him a few inches.

'Is he of small or medium build? Is he a fat man?'

'He's medium,' she said, 'and not fat.' According to her description George could have looked like anybody. The Superintendent was not pleased. He dismissed his men and told them to report to the station. She noticed that they left this time by the front door. There was no longer any need for their discretion. They had enough evidence to leave a house like gentlemen.

When they had gone, the Superintendent sat on George's desk chair, as if meaning to stay, and he motioned her to sit down.

'You seem to be reluctant to give me information, Mrs Verrey Smith,' he said. He reminded her of the stereotype telly detective, a good sort at heart, with a wife and kids of his own, who despite a rough exterior had a deep understanding of human problems. This understanding, he was about to jettison in Mrs Verrey Smith's direction, and she was determined not to be influenced by it.

'You give me the impression that you are holding something back, something perhaps about your husband of which you are ashamed. It is very important for us to find your husband if only for the one reason of clearing his name. I have to tell you, Mrs Verrey Smith, there is obvious suspicion attached to him. It seems from what I have gathered from the other members of the staff, especially from Miss Price, and the Reverend Baines himself, that your husband was very friendly with Mr Parsons, indeed a mite too friendly, as the headmaster put it.' He was referring to his notes again. 'Now there is obviously some connection. It is just possible that your husband has some information that will lead us to an arrest. It is of vital importance that we find him, Mrs Verrey Smith, and it is in your interest that you co-operate with us.'

'I am holding nothing back,' she said. 'I want to see my husband as much as you. My husband was not a secretive man. He told me everything. I have never heard him mention Mr Parsons in this house, and he certainly never came here. My husband is a meek and gentle man and he would not hurt anybody. He must be ill. It's the only explanation I can think of.'

'You contradict yourself, Mrs Verrey Smith,' the Superintendent said. 'You say your husband was not secretive, yet he managed to keep women in his room of whom you knew nothing. You have said your husband is in the best of health, yet you offer the suggestion that he might be ill. I am entitled,

126

Mrs Verrey Smith, to feel that you are withholding something from me.'

She had to invent something that would satisfy him. She had to allay his suspicions. 'Well, frankly, Superintendent,' she said, 'my husband sometimes got very depressed.'

'Was he violent?'

'Oh, no,' she protested. 'Nothing like that. He retired into a shell. Sometimes in such a mood, he would go out and not return till the morning. He would walk for hours and hours. I never knew where he went.'

'Does his doctor know of this?'

'No,' she said quickly. 'He didn't want treatment. He didn't want anybody to know. He thought he might be going mad, and he was worried about his job. He had no friends. No one close, that is. I didn't want to tell you all this. Somehow it's private between me and George. There's a history of insanity in his family,' she elaborated, 'we've always been frightened of it. That's why we had no children.' She felt she had acquitted herself rather well, and the Superintendent, making copious notes, seemed satisfied. She had put him on to the scent of an innocent and gentle lunatic, and in order to authenticate her story, she added, 'Superintendent, I hope that what I'm telling you is confidential.'

He smiled, gratified that yet again, that warm and human telly understanding of his had won the day. She saw him going back to the station, ringing his good wife to tell her yet again that he'd be late for dinner, calling in his trusted lieutenant, and together sorting out his jigsaw of notes. 'You know, Mrs Verrey Smith,' he said, and she'd heard the script a hundred times before, 'we've got to be a bit of the psychiatrist in this job, and it was clear to me from the start that you needed to tell me something. That's why I sent my men away. We'll find your husband, Mrs Verrey Smith, don't worry. We'll check all the hospitals. He might have been picked up with a lapse of memory. He obviously left with every intention of coming back, if not immediately, then in the near future. His passport, his cheque book prove that. I do not attach all that much importance to the open study door. If he was in a state of

depression, he would be too apathetic to cover his tracks. And as you say, he had nothing to hide. I will be in constant touch with you, Mrs Verrey Smith. Here is a number that will get to me direct. If you should hear anything, a letter, a phone call, any piece of information, no matter how trivial it may seem, please be in touch with me right away. And you can be more than sure it will be absolutely confidential. You may have the newspapers calling, and that is something I can do nothing about. It is best to say as little as possible. They will distort it anyway. You've had a very worrying time, Mrs Verrey Smith,' he said, putting his hand on her arm, 'and perhaps in the next few days there will be greater strain. People will talk, and people will give advice and make suggestions. Some of them will not be pleasant. But you must try to weather them. Tell me, Mrs Verrey Smith,' he said, almost in the same breath, his hand still on her arm, 'would it surprise you if some of those people suggested that your husband was a homosexual?'

She tried to move away from him, but there was the slightest suspicion of a tightening on her arm. 'Nonsense,' she said. 'George? Impossible.' She tried to laugh, but deep inside her she knew it was not such a remote possibility. But she must not protest too much. Instead, she forced a smile. 'Why do you ask?' she said.

'Your husband told you about the Parsons affair, I presume?'

'Yes,' she stammered. She had said that George was not secretive. He would have to have told her.

'Are you sure he told you?' the Superintendent said, noting the hesitation.

'He mentioned something,' she said. 'I've forgotten now what it was all about.'

The notebook came out again, a sign of the discovery of yet another piece of the jigsaw puzzle. 'Mr Parsons,' he said, 'before his murder, had been suspended from the school for interfering with little boys. Did your husband not mention that?'

'No. He said there had been some trouble. That's not the kind of story my husband would ever discuss with me,' she

128

said, on her dignity. 'In any case, what has that to do with my husband?'

'Nothing perhaps,' the Superintendent said, putting his notebook away with unconcealed satisfaction, 'except that your husband was the only member of the staff who defended him.'

'He must have had his reasons,' she said timidly.

'Exactly, Mrs Verrey Smith.'

'My husband is a very sympathetic man. He would understand certain human failings.'

'According to the headmaster, and Miss Price in particular, he seemed to show a very personal understanding of Mr Parsons's problem. Now all this may mean nothing at all, but it must all be taken into consideration. Now, Mrs Verrey Smith,' he said, relaxing for the first time his hold on her arm, 'would it surprise you if someone were to suggest that your husband was a homosexual?'

'I think it's a nonsensical suggestion,' she insisted. 'I know my husband very well. You couldn't be married to a man for seventeen years without getting to know him a little. It's a preposterous and ridiculous idea,' she said. 'There can be no truth in it whatsoever.'

He picked up his hat from the desk. 'I hope you will keep in touch with me,' he said again. 'Any information that comes your way. I shall come again tomorrow,' he said.

'Why?' she asked angrily. 'I've told you all I know.'

'I accept that, Mrs Verrey Smith,' he said, 'but by tomorrow, I may have something to tell *you*.'

She followed him down the stairs, and let him out of the front door. Across the road and along the street, she could see a line of half-raised net curtains. She slammed the door in front of them, and went herself into the front room, drawing her net curtains wide, and opening the window to see what they expected to view from theirs. Together they watched the Superintendent's car, with the legend POLICE, blatantly on its roof, take off down the road and turn into the main street.

She returned to the kitchen. The Parsons story had been a great blow to her, not only for its matter but for the fact that George had not mentioned it. It seemed that every finger pointed towards him. She saw him hunted, and she prayed that he trusted her enough to contact her somehow so that she could protect and conceal him. He might phone. If he were alive, he had to contact her.

When the phone rang, she knew it was he, and she sprang to it with a burst of love. 'George?' she panted into the receiver.

It was Mrs Bakewell. 'Are you all right, dear?' she said, having no doubt witnessed the departure of the police.

Mrs Verrey Smith gritted her teeth, and totally mindful of her strait-laced upbringing, she screamed with passion into the receiver, 'Mrs Bakewell, you interfering old bitch, you'd do me a favour if you'd kindly piss off.' She slammed the phone down, and sat again at the table not knowing whether or not she felt any better.

4

Emily Price woke up to the eleven o'clock chimes and a knock on her door. She knew that for some reason, it would take longer than usual to become conscious of who, where and why she was. Yet she knew that the knocking on the door demanded attention. As she got out of bed, she noticed that she was fully dressed and the manner of her dressing startled her. 'Who is it?' she called, and she heard a man's voice emerge from the crumpled silk. So she coughed as a cover, and then repeated the question a pitch or so higher.

'You're wanted on the phone, Mrs Price.'

'Can you take a message?' she said almost squeaking. 'I'm still asleep. I'll phone back.'

She heard the maid going downstairs and she sat on the bed. She had to have a few moments to acclimatize herself. The shock of her dress was sliding away, and there was instead a growing familiarity with her name and whereabouts. There remained only the phone call, and who possibly could know her name and where she was. Then she remembered the man at the station. Possibly it was his mother. She would get the message when she went downstairs, but now she had to wash and tidy herself. She looked very crumpled and there were dirty streaks in her make-up. Somehow she had to go out and buy replacements, and perhaps arrange to have her dress ironed. But with all the small worries, she could not ignore a rousing feeling of well-being. She thought of London, the school and her wife, and all, except for the latter, without a tinge of regret. For her wife, she felt a slight pity but an undeniable affection. She convinced herself that things were better this way, that Joy, a woman, a woman one could have as a friend, would in time, get over it, and begin a new life somehow. She wondered without much curiosity what had happened to Parsons and little Tommy. But the distance between herself and their problems gave her relief, and she knew that in time she would forget them. She was fascinated by the way in which her thinking patterns had changed, and she marvelled that it could make such a difference to one's attitudes. As Emily Price, and she had almost forgotten what her name had been once, she saw Joy as a woman would see her, in anguish and in sorrow. This feeling of compassion came quite naturally. What was strange, and more difficult to accommodate, was the anger she felt towards the person who had been the cause. For Emily Price, who embodied both cause and effect of the situation, harboured in herself and at times in himself, both pity and rage. And yet, as she thought about it, she felt neither witness nor partici-pator, but rather as a catalyst. She saw Joy at home venting her grief on poor old Spit and Polish, and the man who had caused it all was nowhere pointable, not in London, and cer-tainly not in Brighton, but perhaps in the earth with her father. She trembled. Supposing she ever wanted to return? In what form could she stand against the blackboard or in the marital bed? The trousers and jackets lay in her suitcase, but now they could only clothe a ghost, and for a moment she thought of returning, quickly and trousered, before the ghost was finally laid. The decision to become Emily Price had not positively been taken. It had grown on her over the years, and finally in that little chapel, had fixed itself. Now she had to have the courage of that involuntary decision, and she was torn, not knowing what she wanted or needed, and only aware of the perils of both. She half decided that a decision was no longer possible. The making of it had been involuntary, and so had to be its execution. So she smoothed down her dress and tidied up her face, and went downstairs with a little excitement to collect the telephone message.

It was from a Mrs Jumble, and she remembered that that was the name on the card the young man had given her. The young man had lost no time, she thought, in affecting an intro-duction, and there was something suspicious about his haste.

132

But no matter. Mrs Jumble wished Mrs Price to call on her that afternoon at Hove to take tea. She folded the card in her hand and felt that she already had a job and accommodation, and so she decided to rig herself out a little more smartly, not forgetting a handbag, to present herself to Mrs Jumble as a prospective employee. She passed by a newspaper stand, and having passed it, hesitated. In the old days, long ago in her psyche, a morning paper on the way to school was part of the ritual. Now it seemed inappropriate to buy a paper. Ladies, and especially widows, had their morning papers delivered, and she would arrange it for Mrs Jumble if such arrangement were not already effective. She had tea in a small café without drawing anyone's attention, and she spent the morning adding the necessities to her sparse wardrobe. On her return to her hotel, she ordered her dress ironed, had a bath and thoroughly rehabilitated herself. She regretted that she had not bought a newspaper, for she had nothing to do until the afternoon. And it was uncomfortable for her to be unoccupied. She would question the decision that had come upon her. Again she would wonder whether she should reverse it. She even thought that she might write a letter to Joy to say that she was at least alive, but she knew that that kind of action would be equivocal, would betray an infirmity of purpose. To refrain from action was sometimes more positive.

She picked up a Bible that lay on the bedside table. She had not opened a Bible since her childhood, when it had been very much opened for her, night after night, and every Sunday, and thundered into her frightened ear. Now the book evoked an aching nostalgia, but she was unable to outline the participant of the childhood experience. Yet she remembered the joy of being a chorister, and the pretty clothes that she had to wear. She put the Bible down. She could not bear its uneasy promptings. She thought she might take a walk, but the sea unnerved her, and she wondered why she had chosen Brighton to reside, which was, after all, only the sea's interruption. It was perhaps because of the mention of Parsons's fiancée, it she ever existed, but more probably it was because it was not far from the decision that had overtaken her, and therefore more easily reversible. She decided to sleep until the afternoon. In sleep, no decisions nagged, and besides, she wanted again that joyful feeling of awakening, of collecting one's identity out of the dark, of realizing slowly, that you were what you wanted to be.

'Yes, you will do very nicely,' said Mrs Jumble, as she opened the door. It was a greeting that Emily Price had hardly expected. She had waited for a full five minutes at Mrs Jumble's door before ringing, unaware that she was being fully inspected by Mrs Jumble through field glasses fixed on the bedroom window. She had passed the test through a glass darkly, and Mrs Jumble had opened the door to give her the result.

'Come in,' she said. 'The kettle's boiling.'

If the nature of the greeting had been a surprise, it was nothing to what met Emily Price when she entered Mrs Jumble's living-room. The room itself was unimportant, except in so far as it existed to house a large tent which was the living-room proper. What remained of the room was for comings and goings, that were negotiated between four fans, placed at regular intervals around the tent, turning a cold north-easterly at full tilt, so that once you had stepped out of the tent, you had the impression that you were already in the open air. Brighton on the sea was apparently not real enough for Mrs Jumble; she had to have her own Brighton in her living-room.

Emily Price instinctively held on to her wig and decided at that moment that her next purchase must be a hat, to give some justification to her head-holding. 'I've just had my hair done,' she said, by way of apology, and she made for the tent opening to get some shelter.

Mrs Jumble followed her inside, and they sat down, both for some reason out of breath, and for the first time, Emily Price was able to get a full front view of her prospective employer.

She looked at her as a woman sometimes looks at another, with an estimation of age, income and education. As to the first, Mrs Jumble looked younger than Joy, but there were indications that she had worn better. Emily was slightly disturbed by her constant thoughts of her wife. Since arriving in Brighton, she had thought of her more often than during their whole marriage. It was as if Joy had become the standard of comparison for all women. Yes she looked younger than Joy, and had probably during her life been much happier. She was slightly built, with what seemed a deceptive frailty about her person. Her face was ruddy-complexioned and very thin, almost emaciated, as if she had not eaten for a long time. Her black hair hung in separate strands, and looked as if it had been combed, if at all, by a fork. Through the strands over her ears were gentle movements of long gold ear-rings. She smiled. 'What you thinking then?' she said. 'You're thinking I'm a gypsy aren't you? And so I am. A gypsy born and a gypsy to die. But in between,' she laughed, 'my husband was good to me, God bless his soul, but it wasn't like a gypsy marriage. He was in insurance. Fancy. I learned lots of big words. Collateral, premiums,' she laughed, 'but between you and me, I still don't read nor write.'

'How long were you married?' Emily asked, feeling she had to contribute something.

'Twenty-two years. Mind you, I loved him. I was a good wife to him, he'd tell you that himself.' She smiled, recollecting the throttled happiness of their years together. 'But when he passed on, I've got to admit it, I was free again. You can't keep a real gypsy down, Mrs Price, and the day my husband went, I don't mind telling you, I started to live.'

Emily felt an uneasy recognition in her story. Their similar rebirth excited her, but though tempted, she was in no position to give in exchange such intimate confidences. But she warmed to Mrs Jumble. She was a woman who knew exactly who she was, and who had totally and happily concurred with her identity.

'I was brought up in caravans and on commons,' she was saying, 'and when he passed on, God bless him, he left me the house. So I made it my home as best I could. In fact when I was very small. We used to live in a tent from time to time,

135

when they came and took the caravan away. I liked it best of all then.' She stared past Mrs Price without looking at her, and Emily let her be with her memories.

Emily was grateful for the interval. She had been so absorbed by Mrs Jumble's story, the gypsy who had returned to the fold, or tent, as it turned out to be, that she'd had no time to look around the tent itself, though it was evident on first entering, that this was no ordinary camper's site. Being cornerless, it had no set-piece, except perhaps for the green baize table in the centre, dominated by a crystal ball. And it was to this ball that the eye first gravitated and remained, for the whole of the tent and its furnishings were mirrored distortedly in the glass. On top, from the centre pole, swung a bird cage, and a single mournful bird swung with it, having given up the battle for stability long ago. Spit, Emily thought, though again it was a thought of Joy, Spit without his Polish, or vice-versa. Draped in the curves of the circle, were old armchairs, that in reflection took on a deceptive elegance. Spanish shawls draped the backs and arms and astonished red roses bloomed in the glass. There was even a small upright piano, and its two candlesticks curtseyed into the crystal. There was no temptation to look around the tent at the reality, for their distorted reflections seemed to be right and proper. Then her eye fell on her own eye staring into the glass. She felt herself flushing, an entirely new experience for her, and once again she marvelled at the organic difference her dress had made to her bodily function. And then she caught the reflection of Mrs Jumble, staring too, but not into the glass, but into her own reflected eye.

'Now tell me a little about you, dear,' Mrs Jumble was saying.

Emily was totally unprepared, and she hoped that Mrs Jumble would ascribe her hesitation to reticence. She had been called upon without notice to invent the story of a dead husband and for some reason, she thought of the Cloth. If you thought about the Reverend Richard Baines as dead, it was very comforting. 'My husband was in the Church,' she said. 'We were not happy together,' she whispered. It would have been a sad reflection on any human being if they had been

136

happy with the Cloth. 'He was rather a bullying kind, in a Christian sort of way, intolerant and without a great deal of understanding. But he did his best' – it was not done to speak ill of the dead, especially to gypsies – 'but there was a basic incompatibility. He died only six months ago and I sold up in London and decided to come here. My pension is very small, and I have to make a living. But there is a certain freedom without him,' she mused, 'a certain returning to one's real self, as you have done.' She would say no more. She had given a handful of facts that she could contain and remember. Liars had to have good memories, and she knew that hers was shaky. 'I visit his grave twice a month,' she added, more for her own enjoyment than as an extra confidence. The thought of a bi-monthly trample on the Cloth's remains was too tempting to resist.

Mrs Jumble was more than satisfied. 'We have lots in common, I can see,' she said.

The kettle was steaming on a little primus on the floor and Mrs Jumble brewed the tea. They drank it out of tin mugs and she offered biscuits from a packet.

'Tell me about your son,' Mrs Price said, anxious to divert the conversation from herself.

'Bobby's like his father. He's in insurance too, and his life is all planned. He has liver for dinner every Tuesday, and he goes to the pictures every Friday. Things like that. He thinks I'm a bit odd, but I think he's a bit odd too,' she laughed. 'You're looking at my ball,' she said. 'Yes, it's what you think it is. I'm a fortune-teller. Always had a talent for it. My grandmother taught me. I used to do the fairs with her. They say the gift always skips one generation, and it's probably true because my mother had no feeling for it at all. I didn't do it much when my husband, God bless him, was alive. He was against it, called it mumbo-jumbo. But when he died, I built up a small clientele. Regulars, you know. Maybe one day, I'll do yours.'

'I think I'd be rather afraid of that,' Mrs Price said. To tell her fortune would be an acid test of Mrs Jumble's powers, and she was too suspicious of her talent to take the risk. 'Well, one day, perhaps,' she said, 'simply as a friend.'

It was difficult to drink the tea, for the tin mug retained its heat, as well as giving off its own, so Mrs Price could only sip hers slowly and she watched Mrs Jumble as she swallowed hers down and refilled her mug again and again.

'Would you like to stay with me?' she said. 'Share the house, a little company. I couldn't pay you much, but there wouldn't be a lot to do, and I would help you with the cooking.'

Emily wondered how long she could hold down such a job without being discovered. She would be taking many risks. She would actually be living with a woman and there would be little chance of privacy. She hesitated.

'I can give you a lovely bedroom,' Mrs Jumble was saying. 'It was Bobby's room, and it has a bathroom to itself.'

The private bathroom decided it for her. 'Yes,' she said, 'I think I'd like to.'

'Come with me. I'll show you the house,' Mrs Jumble said.

They went first to Mrs Jumble's bedroom. The large marital bed on which Mrs Jumble had been strangled with collaterals stood in the centre of the room, but was easily ignored. For alongside it, strapped to a steel hook on the wall, swung a hammock, attached to the side wall by another hook. A few donkey blankets were draped over it, and as a hangover from her lie-life, a pale blue chiffon nightdress. Mrs Jumble darted towards it, obviously caught out, and stuffed it hurriedly under the blanket, rather as Emily might have hidden her trousers, for both were betrayals of their alien selves.

'This was my mother's bed,' she said, swinging the hammock a little. 'She told me I was born in it, and there, God willing, is where I'm going to die. Now I'll show you your room, or apartments, as my Bobby calls them.'

They walked down a long corridor, and Emily was pleased to note the distance between their two quarters. Bobby's room was very simply furnished, with the bare necessities. It was very much a boy's room, and his school pennants still hung on the wall.

'Needs a woman's hand,' Mrs Jumble said. 'You could make it look very pretty.'

The possibilities of the room thrilled her, though the fact that it was still very much of a boy's room gave her a curious feeling of security. The male room and its female potentialities totally reflected the ambiguity of her own feelings. She would feel very much at home there. She expressed her approval and delight to Mrs Jumble, and they arranged that she should move in on the following morning.

'You would like sheets, I suppose,' Mrs Jumble said doubtfully.

'If you would,' Emily said. 'Just until my boxes arrive from London.' She would deal with those complications later. At the moment, she was content to look forward one day at a time.

On her way back to the hotel, she stopped to buy a London evening paper. She would spend the evening in her room, and she needed a crossword to while away the time, as well as to keep up with what was happening in a world into which she had been newly-born. Was it possible that the world had changed, and that the wars that raged it would touch her differently from before? She had always read the woman's page, even in her other world. Would she now view it with a more critical eye? The newspaper was going to be an exciting adventure, and she wanted to savour it a long time, so she folded it without even scanning the headlines, and hurried back to her hotel.

She took off her shoes, as she had seen Joy do, when she came back from a long and tiring day. She locked the door and took off her wig. It was beginning to feel heavy on her. She was glad that she would have privacy at Mrs Jumble's, and she thought that perhaps occasionally, but only very occasionally, she promised herself, that she would try on her trousers and jacket, just for the bygone feel of it. So she settled herself on the bed, and spread the newspaper wide. The photograph was familiar, too familiar for comfort. She shivered before she recognized it, and wondered why it had made the papers. People disappeared every day without comment from other people, leave alone the Press. She did not want to read about herself, if it was indeed herself, and her abject fear withheld her

139

certainly. She wanted first to study the picture, so she folded the paper round, framing the photograph on its four edges. Now it was less familiar, and she was able to see it as a woman might see it, with approval or otherwise. There was a strange look about the man, a haunted look, pursued as it were, from within. It was a wrong face, as a bull's face on a cow's would be wrong. It was a face full of disturbance. The man was frightened. From both inside and out, he was being pursued. In terror, she had to conclude that it was a face that was wanted for murder. She felt her bowels weaken, and wondered at her panic. Fearfully she spread the paper, and forced herself to read what she had done.

She had merited a sub-headline, but large enough, and direct. 'Have you seen this man?' it challenged, and a cold fear swept through her. Underneath, she had earned a paragraph. 'George Verrey Smith, who disappeared from his home in North London yesterday, is wanted in connection with inquiries into the murder of Samuel Parsons, whose body was found in a school playground in London late last night.' There followed a description of his person, and she was relieved to read that there were no distinguishing marks. Yet the fear gripped her, with a certain incredulity. So she read it again and aloud, and what came out of her throat was the George Verrey Smith voice, and for a moment she panicked that Emily Price had fled for ever from fear. She went on reading as if in self-inflicted punishment. 'He is forty-two years old,' she missed the lack of hesitation, 'with brown eyes and black hair. He is slightly built and was wearing grey flannel trousers with a sports jacket. Any information of his whereabouts should be given immediately to your local police or to Scotland Yard.'

She dropped the paper and stood up, outraged. 'How dare they,' she said to herself, and she saw with undeniable certainty how earnestly the fingers were pointing at her, Miss Price's, the Cloth's, the Staff, even Joy. And at the thought of her, she knew that she had to contact her. Having made that decision, she gave her first thought to Parsons, and she pitied him. She had no notion of how he had met his end. She recalled seeing him behind the shed – it was probably shortly before he died – and she hoped that Washington Jones had gone and that Parsons had died at least buttoned. She had much to tell the police, much that would have helped them. She and Washington Jones were probably the last to see him alive. But she couldn't go back, yet the implications of her continued absence were perilous. She had, in any case, to contact Joy. She put on her wig again, her hands trembling.

Outside in the street, she did not rehearse what she would say, but it had to be Emily Price who was phoning, and no other. There was no going back on that decision. The phone box on the corner was occupied, and gave her unwanted time to think about what she would say. She had to take the risk that her home phone was being monitored, that perhaps the house was full of police. But whatever the circumstances, she had to talk to Joy, not only for her own sake, but for her wife's, whose pain and anguish cut through her. The box was now free, and she went inside, giving herself a few moments to collect her panic-scattered thoughts. Then she dialled the number. The phone was picked up immediately, and she knew that Joy had probably sat up all night and day waiting for such a call.

'Hullo?' It was Joy's voice. The voice made Emily tremble, and it was all she could do to remember her voice pitch and to press it home through the receiver.

'Hullo,' she said. 'Can I speak to Mrs Verrey Smith?' The name astonished her, and she tried not to hear the fear panting over the line.

'Mrs Verrey Smith speaking.'

'My name is Mrs Emily Price,' she said, loud and clear, not confident enough in the name to have to repeat it. 'I'm a friend of your husband's.'

'Where is he?' Joy shouted. It was not just a question. It was an expression of terrible anger, a release of pent-up pain, a flood of concern, and above all, a searing jealousy. 'Are you with him?' she asked, and the 'with' meant bed and betrayal.

Such an interpretation had not occurred to Emily Price and she was totally unprepared to handle it.

'Not, it's not like that at all,' she said, playing it off the cuff.

'We've only just met, and he wants me to get a message to you. He's well,' she went on quickly, 'and he says that one day he'll explain everything. But he wants you to know he had nothing to do with Parsons. Nothing at all. Nothing.' She paused, listening to her own desperation. 'That's all he wanted me to tell you.'

'Where is he?' Joy whispered, as if she was being overheard. 'Where are you speaking from? Why can't I speak to him?'

Her pain was torture to hear. 'He told me,' Emily said, 'to tell you he loves you and he always will.'

'Tell him,' Joy was weeping now, 'tell him, I'll do anything for him. Tell him that. And Mrs Price – look after him, please.'

'I'll do that,' Emily said.

'Will you phone me again?'

'Yes, but say nothing about the calls. I'll phone when I can.'

'Why did he go away?' she begged.

'I don't think he knows himself,' and Emily said it with feeling.

'Will he come back?' she pleaded.

'He doesn't know. He doesn't want to think about it.'

'If he's innocent he's got to come back. Otherwise it makes it worse for him.'

'Yes, I know,' she said, 'but for that reason itself he cannot come back.' She put the phone down quickly, before Joy could argue, and she stayed in the box to steady herself. The decision to leave her old life had been involuntary. It had happened to her from outside. Likewise, the decision to return was not hers either. The police had decided that she could not go back. She felt suddenly trapped, and doubly trapped. George Verrey Smith had trapped her in the trap of Emily Price, and in return she had trapped him. There was no way out for either of them.

Back at the station, the Superintendent, having checked the source of the call, took off his headphones.

'Brighton,' he expostulated, as it rang a thousand bells. Parsons had a fiancée in Brighton. The school staff had told him. So that was it. George Verrey Smith had killed Parsons, and had gone off with his fiancée. It all fitted. The motive was clear. 'Find the woman,' he said to his trusted lieutenant, 'and she will lead us to the man.' So Brighton was their next stop, and Mrs Emily Price, their quarry.

5

Emily Price went quickly back to the hotel. She felt uncomfortable and for the first time since her change, her clothes irritated her. Once in her room, she undressed completely, and naked, she felt free. She avoided the mirrors and stood central in the room. Now she was nothing, neither him nor her. She had stripped into a limbo where possibly her true identity lay. She wondered what she should do. She didn't want to put on the dress again, or the wig, or any of the trappings of her chosen self. She looked at her silk dress and she shivered, partly from chill, but more from repulsion. She reached into her suitcase for something to cover herself. She found herself trousered, and the shirt followed. And then, though warm now, the jacket as well. Automatically she reached for the shoes and socks. She stood up, fully dressed, tingling with a relief that surprised her. Until she looked in the mirror, and she saw the man they were looking for to help them with their inquiries. They had trapped her into that now loathed silk dress and its security. Mrs Jumble was now out of the question. She couldn't read a newspaper, it's true, but she had television, and people talked. It was too much of a risk. And there was Bobby her son. He had seen her, talked to her, read the papers. In time, he might make the connection. She had to get out of Brighton. She had to get some money. She had to get a job. She had to go on living, and in a guise that was no longer pleasurable. A deep longing for George Verrey Smith came over her. She took off his clothes with care, and folded them tenderly into the suitcase. She intended in time to come back to them, and to stay with them for ever. Only the wig she would keep from her present trappings. That would be enough to appease part of her father's ghost. And as for him, that rotten old father of hers, well, she would take him along too. If only she could get back to her study, her sundays, her school, even her wife, all her erstwhile fiction. Hers was the choice after all between the lie and the fantasy, and the latter, after hard wear, tended to wear very thin. She put on her Emily clothes again with loathing. She knew she had to, no longer from any secret appetite, but because it was her only security. The Law compelled the fraud. She counted out her money. Her extravagance on make-up, the last she swore she would ever buy, had put her back in her finances. Now she had only enough to pay for the hotel and sustenance for two or three days more. She closed the case down and checked out at reception. 'A mysterious lady,' the proprietor said to his wife, 'who came and went without reason.'

Outside it was dark, and she was glad of it, for it was yet another disguise. She waited at the bus stop on the promenade, determined to keep to the coast. Inland lay London, and the cities; any place away from the sea was a halt. The coastline was infinite as a circle. On the bus, she took the maximum ticket, which would take her to Worthing. She was careful to speak to nobody, even though the lady by her side smiled at her, and would have been happy to exchange a few words. She too, from her ticket, was going to Worthing, and as soon as the bus emptied a little, Emily Price moved to a seat on her own, where nothing was expected of her.

At the end of the line, she got out and looked around. It was quite dark now, and she knew that she must not stand still for long, in case she risked another Bobby-like encounter. So she moved forward purposefully, but with no direction in mind. It was a warm evening, and she wanted to stay in the air for a while. Besides, she was loathe to go to a boarding-house, and negotiate any kind of arrangement in speech. She didn't trust her Emily voice any more, because her heart was no longer in it. Yet she had to keep in practice, for until her innocence was proved, and God knew how or when, she was stuck with the mezzo-forte contralto, of which she had once been so proud. So she began talking to herself, outlining the items of evidence that weighed against her, and they bred like a snowball, and she was forced to prepare a defence, and it amounted to nothing except a complete denial that had absolutely no proof to support it. In answers to questions of who she was, where and why she was there, she gave no reply, because all that had nothing to do with anything. It was a pretty poor defence, she knew, and she found herself making it to the sea, where she had arrived without intent. She hoped she would not be seen. A black-clad, middle-aged lady, traipsing across the sands at night, carrying a suitcase, would be an object of suspicion in any circumstances. She hurried over to the rocks where there was shelter. She found a cave with a natural rock seat as its base, and she put down her case and considered what to do. She was hidden there and safe. The water never came that far. She would sleep there and spend what money she had on food. She dared not think of the future. What had already become of her was enough. She looked down at her dress. It was crumpled, and at the seams, already frayed. She thought of Ethel. She had been right. It wasn't a good buy, but then, as she herself had said, but for different reasons, she wasn't buying for durability. She didn't regret that the dress was wearing out. She had come to loathe its necessity, and all that it stood for. She looked around her, avoiding her clothing. She couldn't stay in this cave for ever. She looked at the sea, and it roared back at her like an inquisitor. She turned her back, and staring into a jugged slab of rock, she tried not to think of who she was, neither in her terms nor in theirs, for she knew that both were unreliable.

6

The Superintendent sent his trusted lieutenant to Brighton to carry out the initial ferreting. He himself would arrive for the kill. Besides, he had to complete routine investigations in London. He had not yet visited Parsons's lodgings. His landlady had come to identify the body, but he knew nothing of the way Parsons had lived. For the Superintendent, the visit was a formality only. In his mind, George Verrey Smith had done the job and his motive was very clear. Verrey Smith had probably been after Mrs Price for some while. It was possibly she who had spent a furtive night or two in the Verrey Smith study. Things had come to a head when Parsons's little diversions had been revealed. Parsons had proved himself even less worthy of Mrs Price's attentions than Verrey Smith had already supposed. And so Verrey Smith had taught Parsons a lesson, an extreme one to say the least. The Superintendent knew there were certain factors in his solution that could not be accounted for. Verrey Smith's reported friendship with Parsons, and his alleged defence of the murdered man. But apart from those two factors, everything else fitted. The Superintendent liked his solution, and he expected to make an arrest within the week.

Parsons lived near the school. It was a bed and breakfast arrangement, with full meals at the weekends. Mrs Jenkins, his landlady, did for other gentlemen besides Parsons. All professional people, she hastened to tell the Superintendent. 'I don't take anybody and my gentlemen have been with me for years.' Mrs Jenkins was far more concerned with the possible stain on the reputation of her establishment, than she was for the loss of a tenant, a highly replaceable commodity in view of the waiting list that clamoured for vacancies. There was very little

Mrs Jenkins could contribute to her late gentleman's character, except that he was, like all her gentlemen, quiet and decent – Mrs Jenkins obviously knew nothing about the maintenance shed – and that he kept himself to himself.

'Did he have any visitors, Mrs Jenkins? Any colleagues from the school perhaps?'

'No one from the school,' Mrs Jenkins said, 'I don't think he had any proper friends there. Kept things apart you know. Come four-thirty, and school was over.'

'How did he spend his evenings, and his weekends?'

'Well, I'm not a one to pry, Inspector,' she said. 'He had a fiancée in Brighton, he told me, and I think he spent most weekends there. He had a regular visitor every Friday night. A Mr Chipple. Jolly man. He never stayed very long. But he was a regular. Every Friday.'

'D'you know anything more about this Mr Chipple? Where he lived? What he did for a living?'

'I make it my business not to interfere with the private lives of my gentlemen, Inspector,' she said. 'That's all I know about him. Just his name and what he looks like.'

'How d'you come to know his name, Mrs Jenkins, since you are not the interfering type?'

Mrs Jenkins sneered. 'He's been coming here every Friday for the past four years. Ever since Mr Parsons, the late Mr Parsons I should say, moved in, in fact. Used to answer the door to him myself, sometimes. But that's all I know about him.'

'How long did he stay on a Friday?'

'I didn't time him, Inspector. What my gentlemen do, and for how long they do it, is their own business.'

Mrs Jenkins was beginning to wear the Superintendent down. He was irritated by her desperate respectability. He couldn't imagine how anyone could stay there. Mrs Jenkins was giving away nothing, possibly because she had nothing to give, but she was certainly making a virtue of it. Parsons had no relatives, and it seemed, apart from Mr Chipple and his Brighton fiancée, no friends. The Superintendent's whole interest was focused on Brighton, and Mr Chipple was an irritat-

148

ing irrelevancy, who would no doubt show up and be accounted for. The other gentlemen in the house had had little to do with Parsons, and had even less than Mrs Jenkins to offer. All this, the Superintendent was sure, was a waste of time. There was Parsons's room to be examined, and after that he himself would take off for Brighton after his key witness.

Mrs Jenkins led the way up the stairs. 'Do not' notices were everywhere, referring to rubbish, lights, taps and visitors, interspersed with 'God is Love' and 'Home sweet Home', further threats to the intimidated lodger. Parsons's room revealed very little that added to the Superintendent's picture of the murdered man. It was scrupulously clean and tidy. An unfinished crossword puzzle lay on the table alongside a prepared draughts board, obviously, the Superintendent concluded, his regular Friday occupation with Mr Chipple. Then there was Parsons's desk, with his papers neatly arranged in cubby holes. 'I would like to go through his papers, Mrs Jenkins,' the Superintendent said. 'I shan't be needing you.'

Mrs Jenkins made no move. 'I'm responsible for my gentlemen's belongings,' she said.

'Your gentleman has been murdered, Mrs Jenkins. His belongings are no longer your responsibility. The police have the right to investigate wherever they feel it is necessary. I shall not need you here.'

'I don't like doing this, Inspector,' she said.

'I will take full responsibility, Mrs Jenkins.'

She sulked out of the room, straightening the late Mr Parsons's already straight counterpane.

The Superintendent started to go through the papers. There were no letters of any relevance, or notebooks. There were collections of postcards of old master reproductions, purchased from the National Gallery. There were cellophane packets of foreign stamps and semi-precious stones. And there was his bankbook, statements and cheques. The Superintendent went through these thoroughly, though with little heart, for his thoughts were itching for Brighton, but after a perusal of Parsons's accounts, he was bound to admit that Parsons drew an inordinately large sum every week, considering his comparatively frugal way of life. It was a clue he could not in all conscience dismiss. He packed the accounts into his brief-case and went downstairs.

On his way back to the station, he tried to find some innocent explanation of the large withdrawals. The obvious answer, which in any other case, the Superintendent would have reached for, was possible blackmail, but his thinking was so fixedly pointed in George Verrey Smith's direction, and to his obvious motive, that he would not admit of this possibility. So he decided with equal logic that Parsons was keeping Mrs Price in Brighton, and that the extra cash was for her rent and board. He was delighted with his reasoning, and hurried back to the station to collect any new developments. There was nothing from Brighton – he didn't, in any case, expect news so soon. He plugged in his headphones to hear if Mrs Verrey Smith had anything new to offer. There had been two calls, one that Mrs Verrey Smith had made herself; a pathetic apology to a Mrs Bakewell for verbal insults tendered, which ended in an invitation to tea from the latter to prove that she, Mrs Bakewell, knew the meaning of true friendship. The second call announced Mrs Verrey Smith's great and good fortune in having been chosen to receive six free dancing lessons from the Rainbow Teaching Establishment, and Mrs Verrey Smith's not surprising, if rather vociferous, refusal. He took his headphones off. It was early days. He was not dissatisfied.

7

It was now the seventh day of his disappearance, and Joy Verrey Smith was losing hope of ever seeing him again. Apart from a hurried cup of tea at Mrs Bakewell's, to whom she had confided all that Mrs Bakewell already knew from the papers, she had not left the house since George's disappearance. He had not phoned again, but she hadn't given up hope, and every time the phone rang, which was rarely, she rushed to the receiver in a burst of anger and forgiveness. But such calls as she had received had merited neither. Apart from the news reporters, few people had come to see her. Some neighbours had offered to do her shopping and laundry. Mrs Johnson had opted to stay with her own mourning, and for that Joy Verrey Smith was grateful.

The house was quiet and dirty. Over the Georgeless days, it had accumulated dust and dishes, and a mountain of cigarette ends. Spit and Polish were suddenly misnomers, their brass cage tarnished and lack-lustre, and their occasional songs likewise. As the days passed, the newspaper coverage lessened, so it was less of an agony to pick up the morning's paper from the doormat. But today, a letter had come with it, and she sat at the kitchen table looking at it, as she had done for the last two hours, not daring to open it for she sensed that it contained a clue that might undo her. It was a familiar handwriting, and a familiar postmark. Ireland. A letter had come for George from Ireland every week and, though she had always been curious, she had never dared to refer to it. Only once, and it was the first time such a letter had arrived, had she asked George about it, and he was so outraged by her interference that she had said no more. But every week she had slid the letter under his study door, and tried to forget about it, till the next one arrived. Now there was no delivery room, and no one but herself to open it. She dreaded that it would reveal a story of which she had been happily ignorant until now. But she knew she had to open it, sooner or later. It could well be a clue, not to his present disappearance, but to the reasons why he went at all.

She covered Spit and Polish's cage. The letter was strictly private. Once again she read the sender's address on the back of the envelope. It was the same as it had been over the years, but there was no name attached. She was careful not to tear into it as she opened the letter. She waited for a while before taking the letter out, for a sign perhaps that she should not do it, for a ring at the doorbell, or the telephone, or a scream from Spit or Polish. But there was nothing in the silent house to stop her.

She took the letter out and spread it on the table. It was written in an ominous purple. The address was given again on the top righthand corner, printed this time, but underlined in purple ink. The message was short. Great pains had been taken with its lay-out; the margins between the florid purple were equal, and the whole message was central to the page. As a piece of calligraphy it was pleasurable to view, until you came to the matter of the message, which was, to say the least, alarming. 'CONFESS, CONFESS' it read, 'my son', half of it in bold capitals, and the rest, which carried less confidence, in small purple letters. That was all. She read it many times. Backwards and forwards, even up and down, the message was the same, and all ways, abundantly clear. So George had done it, and somehow his mother knew. George was Parsons's murderer, and a mother was pleading with her son to give himself up. She had to see her. They had had no contact since Mrs Verrey Smith had moved to Ireland on her re-marriage. But they were not on non-speaking terms. She had to find out what George's mother knew about Parsons, how she had found out, and what story lay behind it all. How could the mother be so sure that George was a murderer? She had to see her. But she couldn't go to Ireland. The Superintendent would be suspicious of the move, and besides, she couldn't leave the phone. No,

Mrs Verrey Smith, or whatever she was now called, was going to have to come to her. She could send her a telegram. She didn't want to do it over the telephone. It would be checkable, and in any case, she couldn't be too sure that her phone was not tapped. The Superintendent had come to visit her every day, and he had not mentioned Brighton. Had he heard the call, he would surely have gone there. But she could not be too sure. She would go to the Post Office. She hated leaving the phone, so she took off the receiver. George would ring again. She didn't want him to think that the house was empty, or he might feel utterly betrayed. So she hurried, and at the Post Office counter she thought for the first time how to word the telegram. 'George in desperate trouble,' she tried. 'Come at once.' But it sounded by way of an order, and she wanted more of a plea. So she emended it a little. 'George in desperate trouble,' she decided. 'He begs you to come at once.' Such a message, she felt sure, could not be denied. She handed it furtively over the counter, but there was no untoward reaction from the assistant. Not even a nod of sympathy, and Joy Verrey Smith was glad of it. She hurried home and replaced the receiver. For the first time, she noticed how dirty the house was and, prompted by the possible visit of her mother-in-law, she decided that, George or no, she must clean it up. She went about it with an energy that surprised her. She polished the bird cage till it shone, and Spit and Polish gratefully offered a *Te Deum*. When it was all done, she saw to herself. She bathed and changed, and tried to feel much better. She was pinning all her hopes on George's mother to unravel the mystery, but it nagged at her that, when all was said and done, she had married a murderer.

When the front doorbell rang, she supposed it was the Superintendent, and she feared that she might have been followed to the Post Office, and her message discovered. But it was a woman's shadow, which turned out in substance to be Mrs Johnson.

Joy Verrey Smith opened the door, but made no gesture of inviting her in. Mrs Johnson, on her part, was rather surprised, since she had come merely as a neighbour to offer what help she could. She obviously did not know of Tommy's tales, or she dared not have come. Mrs Verrey Smith hesitated. Perhaps there was no truth in it at all, and here was a woman, ripe herself in mourning, come to console her. She asked her in, glad now that the house was clean, and they went into the kitchen.

'I don't know what to say to you,' Mrs Johnson said. 'If there's anything I can do. You were so good to me in my trouble.'

'How's Tommy?' Mrs Verrey Smith asked. She still had a nagging concern for her possible stepson, though he did tend to look like the late Mr Johnson. She looked closely at his mother and wondered what, if anything, George had seen in her. She was much too tall for any practical purpose, and much too angular to be called attractive. 'Did you know George well?' she asked.

She noticed that Mrs Johnson did not flinch at the question.

'Not well,' she said. 'I didn't see very much of him, except occasionally on his way to school in the mornings. Did he have any close friends?'

'Not that I knew of,' Joy said. 'He was very secretive, you know.' For some reason, she felt herself warming towards the woman, possibly because of their common bereavement, but she envied Mrs Johnson the finality of her loss, and the stainless reputation her husband had managed to take with him. 'He couldn't have done it,' she said suddenly. 'George couldn't hurt anybody.'

'He struck me as being very kind and gentle,' Mrs Johnson agreed, though it was contrary to all the reports of him that Tommy brought home from school. But she cared not to reveal that she had had personal experience of his kindness. She wondered whether Mrs Verrey Smith knew, and whether that accounted for her initial hesitation at the front door. 'It's a terrible mistake,' she said. 'The fact that he disappeared at the time of the murder doesn't mean anything. People disappear every day. Don't let's talk about it if you don't want to, dear.' She put her hand on Joy's arm.

'No, it helps to talk about it,' Joy said. 'But I don't know what to say. I don't know anything about anything, except that he isn't here and that he's been gone for over a week, and there hasn't been a word from him.'

'You'll hear, I'm sure you'll hear. He must be alive, or you would have heard by now. Try not to worry. I know it's easy to say. It's a terrible nightmare. But it will pass.'

They sat for a while in silence. Joy wondered whether she should bring up the Tommy business, but she decided against it. If it were not true, then it need not be spoken about, but if Tommy were her stepson, she did not want it known that she knew, for she would have to effect a reaction that might change her whole life. In any case, it was best to wait for George's return, and at that thought, she shivered.

The Superintendent came while they sat there, and asked to see Mrs Verrey Smith privately. Mrs Johnson took her leave, with promises to return with a cooked supper.

'You have good neighbours,' the Superintendent said when she was gone. Having made a polite beginning, he thought he might as well come straight to the point. 'You promised to be in touch with me if you heard anything, Mrs Verrey Smith.'

She trembled. They were tapping her phone. She gave herself time to count her luck that she had gone to the Post Office to send the wire to Ireland. 'I don't know what you mean,' she said.

'About a week ago, you had a phone call from Brighton, Mrs Verrey Smith. Your telephone is monitored at the station.'

'Why?' she said angrily. 'Don't you trust me?'

'You have given me little cause,' he said. 'What are you trying to hide? My men are in Brighton now. We shall find Mrs Price, Mrs Verrey Smith, I assure you. But you owe it to us to give us any information. Have you heard from your husband since, or from Mrs Price, by letter, perhaps, or a message? Think carefully. Have there been any letters that might give us a clue?'

'No,' she said quickly. 'I haven't heard anything from Mrs Price or my husband.'

'It was clear from the conversation that you do not know

Mrs Price,' the Superintendent said. 'These women your husband entertained in his study. Did you know any of them?'

'No,' she said. It was true, because there had never been any.

'I don't want to intercept your letters, Mrs Verrey Smith,' he said quietly.

'I'm hiding nothing,' she said. 'I didn't tell you about the phone call because I'm concerned first of all with my husband's safety. Even if he is with another woman. When you find Mr Parsons's real murderer, my husband will come back, and I don't know why you're wasting your time here or in Brighton for that matter, when the real murderer has probably left the country by now.' She was glad to have got it off her chest.

'Your husband is suspect number one. I think you ought to know that, Mrs Verrey Smith, and since he disappeared there are other leads that have come to light that have only served to confirm our suspicions.' He would give her a run for her money. He would say no more.

'What leads?' she whispered.

'At the moment, I cannot divulge that,' he said, 'for they may come to nothing. But if by chance your husband does communicate with you, in some form or another, or perhaps Mrs Price, it would be well if you could let them know that the net is closing.'

She crumpled in her chair.

'Now, Mrs Verrey Smith.' He stood over her. 'Are you still keeping some information from me?'

'I have nothing,' she said. The letter from his mother was no information. It was only an opinion, an opinion that tallied only too well with the Superintendent's. 'Nothing at all. But tell me what the leads are,' she shouted. 'I'm entitled to know. I'm his wife.'

'We have it on good information, Mrs Verrey Smith, that the late Mr Parsons had a fiancée in Brighton. It is too much of a coincidence to be ignored.'

'He went to Brighton because it's near London. That's the only reason he went to Brighton.'

'So is Ipswich, so is Bournemouth, so are a hundred other

places. I don't wish to upset you, Mrs Verrey Smith, but you do your husband no good by hiding information from us. If your husband is innocent, and he may well be innocent, then we have to find him so that he can prove it. You understand, don't you?'

She nodded. What about Tommy's story, she thought? Was that information too? She decided to keep quiet about it. That too was an opinion, Tommy's opinion, like George's mother's; neither could be construed as fact.

As she opened the door for the Superintendent to leave, the net curtains were dropped again, and she wanted to go into the street and kill everybody. Had some such outrageous provocation prompted George with Mr Parsons, and she realized with horror, that with this thought, she had accepted her husband as a murderer.

As she was shutting the door on the Superintendent, the phone rang. Quickly he put his foot back inside. 'Why don't you answer it?' she said. 'Then you can be quite sure, can't you.'

'It's your telephone, Mrs Verrey Smith,' he said.

'It's yours too. At the station. So you might as well answer it here.' She desperately wanted someone to answer it. It might be George, and he would have the sense to put the phone down if a man answered it. And if it were George, and she answered it, what could she say? Yet she dreaded that the phone would stop. Neither made a move.

'If it's an important call,' the Superintendent said, 'they will ring off if I answer it. Whoever is calling wants to speak to you, Mrs Verrey Smith.'

She could stand the bell no longer and she picked up the receiver. Suddenly the Superintendent was close behind her.

'Hullo?' she said.

'Mrs Verrey Smith?' It was a small boy's voice.

'Speaking.'

The Superintendent was now so close that she was forced to share the receiver with him.

'I seen your 'usband's photo in the papers,' the little boy said, 'an it wasn't 'im wot did it, 'cos I saw it.'

157

Mrs Verrey Smith and the Superintendent looked at each other.

'Who are you?' she said frantically. 'What's your name?'

There was a silence the other end. The Superintendent grabbed the receiver. 'Who are you?' he shouted, then more gently, as he collected himself. 'Tell me your name, laddie.'

They heard the click of the receiver.

'There's another lead for you, Superintendent,' Mrs Verrey Smith said. Suddenly she felt free, as if George had been totally acquitted. 'You heard that, Superintendent? Why don't you do something about that,' she said, 'instead of wasting your time in Brighton?'

'We follow every lead, Mrs Verrey Smith. But don't pin your hopes too highly on that call,' he said. 'Whenever a murder is committed lots of cranks come up with stories.'

'But that was a child,' she said. 'He would have given me his name if you hadn't interfered. Now he won't contact me again.'

The Superintendent knew she was right. He had acted hastily. 'He will contact you again,' he said, without conviction. His Brighton feelings were threatened. He couldn't afford to ignore any piece of information, especially from a frightened child. He had to find Verrey Smith. Even if it didn't lead to a conviction, he had to find him.

'Mrs Verrey Smith,' he said. 'We must somehow appeal to your husband to come home. If you perhaps would agree to make a plea on television. I could arrange the time. Who knows, he might see it, or be told about it. It couldn't help but move him.'

The idea startled her, and in it she sensed that the Superintendent had changed his track. He had been thrown by that telephone call. She would co-operate. For the first time she felt that it might be in George's interest, and she would be glad to do something to counteract the terrible message from George's mother.

'Yes,' she said. 'But I'll do the words myself.'

The Superintendent was surprised at her ready agreement, 'Of course, of course,' he said. 'Then I shall make the necessary arrangements.'

She took him once more to the door, and the Superintendent left a distinct air of retreat behind him. For the first time since George's disappearance, Mrs Verrey Smith had hope. She wanted to tell somebody about the phone call. She wanted her hope confirmed by somebody else. But she would give the Superintendent time to get back to the station. Then she would phone Mrs Johnson, and he would have to hear it once again, and this time, laced with her triumph. While waiting, she would content herself with telling Spit and Polish. It seemed that her life was going back to normal. Already she was beginning to put the nightmare behind her. It was now only a question of George's certain return, and dealing, one way or another, with his stupid mother. She recalled the purple message, and tried not to let it shake her hope. Then she saw with horror that she had left it lying open on the kitchen table. She put her head in her hands, and trembled with a criminal's terror of not knowing what was known.

8

Mrs Verrey Smith senior, or Mrs Whitely, as she stressed she had been promoted to, arrived the following morning, with thankfully no warning of her coming, either by wire or telephone. She simply knocked on the front door.

'God be with you,' she said, before even checking on the recipient of her blessing. Then seeing her daughter-in-law, whom she had never closely examined, she said, 'Joy, isn't it?'

They had not seen each other for over ten years, and it was clear that each had found the other, in memory at least, faintly resistible.

'That's right,' Joy said, asking her in. They went into the front room, and Joy went to the window to watch the neighbouring curtains drop. Opposite, a woman was too late, and Joy waved at her. The woman mouthed something, clearly to the effect of 'brazen hussey', and turned away.

'Well, where is he?' Mrs Whitely asked, sitting herself down. 'And what's the trouble?'

Joy was dumbfounded. 'You don't know?' she said. 'Don't you read the papers?'

'Newspapers,' Mrs Whitely scoffed. 'All lies. The Devil's work. What's happened? What's happened to George?'

'But your letter,' Joy said. She had to settle that first. 'Confess, it said. To what? What did it mean?'

'You mean there's someone else? He's killed someone else?' Joy sat down. She didn't know which one of them was mad. And the Superintendent – if he'd seen that letter, God knows what fruity evidence he'd unconsciously collected. Apparently homicide was her husband's hobby. 'What did you mean in your letter?' she tried again. 'Confess to what?'

'I can't tell you about that. That is something between George and his Maker. Now tell me what has happened.'

So Joy told her the bare facts, adding nothing to what the papers had already divulged. And having given her the whole story, as if in total confidence, she demanded in exchange, an account of George's former trespass, as she had a right, as his wife, to know.

Mrs Whitely was not impressed by her claim. 'One has nothing to do with the other,' she insisted. 'Though once set on the downward path, there is little hope of turning back without the help of our Lord. And he never sought that help, though the dear Lord will witness that every week I implored him to seek absolution.'

Well, that at least explained those weekly missives. But the matter of the vital confession remained a mystery to her, and Mrs Whitely was giving away nothing. She thought her mother-in-law showed more curiosity than concern, and that her trip was no doubt of an evangelical nature that was only triggered off by her son's disappearance.

'I don't suppose you have ever encouraged him into the church,' Mrs Whitely said.

'I do a lot of church work. George's religious feelings are not my business.'

'Of course they're your business,' Mrs Whitely said, 'and part of your duties too.' She was all but telling her that she was responsible for the second murder at least. 'Now what are we going to do about it? We have to find him,' Mrs Whitely said, in her best practical manner.

'I don't know what more I can do. I've no idea where he could have gone. I can only hope that he's still alive.'

'We must go to a diviner,' Mrs Whitely said.

'A diviner?'

'You've heard of a water diviner, my dear,' Mrs Whitely said, trying to be patient. 'Well there are people diviners. They tell you the whereabouts of missing persons.'

'But how?'

'Well you give them a description of the person who's gone, and then they hold something belonging to them. A piece of

161

clothing or a watch or something. They can at least tell you if he's alive or not.'

Joy shuddered.

'Well, it's better to know the worst, that's what I think.' Mrs Whitely's tardy re-marriage to the church, and the grand issue she was making of it, seemed to absolve her of all feelings. Dogma would take care of everything. Joy wondered what kind of man was Mr Whitely, and whether he too was totally accounted for in the creed. She found this diviner mumbo-jumbo hard to reconcile with the altar phraseology that dripped from her mother-in-law's lips, and she ventured to suggest that such a pursuit was faintly pagan. 'The police use them, you know,' Mrs Whitely was quick to defend herself. The fact that the Law availed itself of such a facility, made it slightly more kosher. 'There used to be a Mr Wentworth. Lived in Stamford Hill. He'd be in the phone book if he's still alive. Clive Wentworth, that's it. George's father, God rest his soul, used to know him. He used to be quite famous. We could ring him up for an appointment.'

'No, not the phone,' Joy interrupted her, and she explained why her telephone was unusable. So it was arranged that Mrs Whitely should go to the Post Office and phone him from there, if he was still alive. But before she left, she asked to see her room so that she could unpack a few things, which, as Joy watched her, turned out to be very little clothing, but an abundance of church gear. She had even brought her own hammer and nail for her crucifix, which she proceeded to hang on the wall above her bed. Next came a do-it-yourself altar, plastic and painted by numbers. This she set up on the bedside table.

She was obviously relieved to have thus unburdened herself. A holdall was no place for instant religion. She looked around her room and sighed with satisfaction. Now she was ready to face whatever vicissitudes her wayward son had landed her in.

When she had gone, Joy went back into the front room and sprayed it with Fresh-air. Mrs Whitely had brought the mustiness of the church with her, both on her person and in her holdall. Joy Verrey Smith wondered how long she was going to stay.

She heard a car draw up outside, and from the raising of curtains opposite, she knew that something was afoot in the street. It was probably the Superintendent again with questions pertaining to the confession letter. She did not care any more about the Superintendent. Since the phone call from the little boy, George had, in her mind, been acquitted of one murder at least. The other was possibly a figment of his mother's imagination.

She went over to the window to investigate. It was a large van, and the Superintendent's car was parked behind. It was a feast for the neighbours. She opened the door to the Superintendent and the men and their equipment followed him inside.

'This won't take very long,' the Superintendent was saying. 'Shall we do it here?' he said, pointing to the front room. 'Now you just relax, Mrs Verrey Smith. We can discuss what you'll say, while they're getting everything ready.' The Superintendent had taken over the role of director. 'I thought perhaps you would prefer to talk to a reporter, rather than straight to the camera.' He himself was itching for a part in the production, but there was no valid role for him to play. So he busied himself in seating Mrs Verrey Smith and the reporter, checking with the director from time to time as to their positions. After some discussion and much shifting of lights, it seemed that they were ready. The camera-man suggested a little powder on Mrs Verrey Smith's chin to take off the shine, and the director, who had once, many years ago, made a 'B' feature and, apart from the odd day, had been out of work ever since, readily agreed with him, for there was no reason why the interview, though a straighforward piece of reporting, should not be of artistic value. All this set him off on repositioning the lights, so that Mrs Verrey Smith in profile would look rather fetching. 'After all,' he explained to the Superintendent, who by now was getting rather restless, 'here is a woman in distress, appealing to her husband to come home.' Once again, he saw himself in the studios, under the great arc lights, the sound and camera crews hanging on his every word.

'She should rest her chin on her hand, I think,' he said. 'Let me see that position, Mrs Verrey Smith.' He looked through the eye-piece, and found his star satisfactory.

The Superintendent thought the director was overstepping himself. 'It's only an appeal,' he said. 'We're not making a Hollywood spectacular.'

The director ignored him. As far as he was concerned, the Superintendent was a mere clapper-boy and only served to reinforce the atmosphere of crew versus director tension, which, after all, obtains on any production. He motioned the Superintendent to stand behind the camera, or otherwise cast his shadow over the whole proceedings. He then relit the whole scene as for a feature, and after much rearrangement of mikes, lights and camera-positions, he announced himself ready to shoot.

Then the doorbell rang. The Superintendent, knowing his cue, crossed over the set, and in doing so, tripped over one of the cables, bringing a lamp crashing down, and narrowly missing the camera.

'You're fired,' the director shouted, still reigning down in Elstree.

'I'm sorry,' the Superintendent said. 'But nothing is broken. You film people always make such a fuss.' He was out of the room before the director could reply. The crash had brought him sadly back to a parlour in suburban London, to a set that was barely documentary. His job was a mere piece of reportage, that needed only to be in focus, and required no direction whatsoever.

The Superintendent returned with Mrs Whitely. 'You didn't tell me about your mother-in-law,' he said accusingly.

'But she's only just arrived,' Joy said. 'There's no particular significance in her coming. She is anxious for her son. Her arrival, Superintendent, is not information.'

The director was quick to catch the antagonism between these two, and it heartened him a little to feel that he was dealing with a temperamental leading lady.

The Superintendent ignored her. 'I think perhaps I would like Mrs Whitely in the interview,' he said.

The director sat down, overcome by the vicissitudes of his craft. He sighed with the burden of his creativity. 'Perhaps you would like to reposition them, Inspector. Kill the lights,' he ordered. 'We're back to square one.'

And so it started all over again. Mrs Whitely sat next to her daughter-in-law. 'I found him,' she whispered. 'I made an appointment for tomorrow. We must take some of his clothing.'

'Relax, relax,' the director directed his increased cast. He studied Mrs Whitely to see what he could make of her. She had taken off her hat and he decided that she looked more worried with it on. In his book, an anxious mother was hatted, and he asked her to replace it.

'You don't wear a hat in the house,' the Superintendent objected.

'Worried mothers,' the director said with authority, 'wear hats wherever they are.'

'But this is not a – er – movie.'

'Even a straight piece of reporting must carry its own inbuilt appeal, Inspector. Relax, this will take a little while.'

The Superintendent placed himself in the set between Mrs Whitely and Mrs Verrey Smith.

'I can't light the set if you're in it, Inspector. D'you mind sitting just here? Behind the camera.'

The Superintendent moved obediently and, squatting on his haunches, he indulged in a wild fantasy of arresting the whole film-director profession on a charge of mass murder and hanging each one personally. This one, he decided, would drop twice.

It took the rest of the morning to light the set and to prepare for shooting. Then after a hot-dinner break, insisted on by the soundcrew, quoting Article 17b of the Union Rules, the cameras started to roll. It was six o'clock before the 'Wrap' order came. The director had enough film in the can for three hours' viewing. The Superintendent had booked television time for five minutes.

As the crew were leaving, the Superintendent lagged behind. 'I don't suppose, Mrs Whitely,' he said, 'that you have any extra information about where your son would be hiding?'

'We can only pray for guidance,' Mrs Whitely said. 'I pray that we will find him in the bosom of the church. He has much business to do there,' she said, looking at Joy.

The Superintendent shrugged. In his mind he recapped Mrs Whitely's sermon before the cameras, and he wondered whether he could make an extra bob or two by selling the off-cuts to religious broadcasting. It wasn't a bad business, film-making. As he drove off in his car, he thought he might suggest a possible career for his son.

When he got back to the station, the night-shift had already taken over. He thought he would take a train down to Brighton. There'd been no news from there, but he was restless sitting around in London, when he knew, though now with less conviction, that Brighton was a more promising hunting-ground.

He crossed over the foyer to his office. A coloured woman was standing at the reception desk. Her head was pressed on her hand. Her body was shaking; she was obviously in deep distress. The policeman behind the counter was trying to get her particulars, but she was obviously so overwrought, that only a few unintelligible words could escape her. 'I'll handle this, Officer,' the Superintendent said, and he helped the woman into his office. He sat her down, gave her some water and tried to calm her.

'Now what can we do for you?' he said.

'It's my son,' she stammered. 'He's lost. He hasn't come home from school.' She gathered momentum as the information flooded out. 'He's never late. Always back from school at half-past four. He's a good boy. Wouldn't go anywhere without telling me first. He's ten, and he had on a green pullover. His name's Washington. He's my youngest. You've got to find him.'

'Washington,' the Superintendent said. 'Washington what?' He was prepared for an equally exotic surname.

'Jones,' she said flatly, starting to cry again.

The Superintendent could see the last train for Brighton leaving without him. He rang for the senior officer, and instructed him to see to the woman, and if necessary to start a search for the boy. He tapped her shoulder as he left. 'Probably playing football somewhere, Mrs Jones. Nothing to worry about. We'll find him.'

She broke into a new burst of sobbing. He looked at the senior officer and nodded to the jug of water on the desk. When in doubt, or playing for time, use water. He wondered why the film director hadn't used a glass on the set. And that reminded him. He must ring up home to check that his sons were back from school. He decided to do it from the railway station. He was anxious to get away from his office. There was something about this woman that disturbed him deeply. It was always painful when a child was lost, but this woman was sobbing as if already bereaved. He called the senior officer over and whispered to him, 'Get an all-out search for that boy. For some reason or other, I don't like it. Keep me informed. I want him found, and quickly.'

9

The Superintendent's trusted lieutenant had ferreted Brighton for a week, and had come up with nothing. He'd covered all the large hotels, and most of the boarding-houses. There were far too many to cover them all. In any case, Mrs Price was far more likely to be staying as a lodger somewhere, or with friends. 'They've gone underground' was his phrase to cover his failure, and it was his greeting to his chief when he arrived from London. 'Gone underground' was less final than 'totally disappeared'. It held hope for eventual discovery.

The Superintendent was not impressed whatever the phrasing. 'Have you scoured the beaches?' he said. 'They could have taken a boat. Did you make all inquiries?'

The trusted lieutenant, now feeling himself slightly less trusted, nodded. The boat possibility hadn't occurred to him, but he dared not confess to it. He would do it quietly and on his own, in the morning.

'Brighton's not such a big place,' the Superintendent was saying. 'The woman's bound to come out to do her shopping. Are there men in the markets? Have you no leads at all?'

The lieutenant was bound in truth to shake his head.

'I'll patrol myself tomorrow,' the Superintendent said. 'Though they've had a week to slip out of our hands. I should have come here immediately,' he said, almost to himself. 'We've got to find Emily Price,' he said aloud. Now that he felt her slipping from his grasp, he became more and more convinced that she was harbouring a murderer. 'There's a television appeal going out tomorrow,' he said. 'There's bound to be a response,' he almost shouted. He was very tired, and he knew that if he talked much longer he would lose his temper.

He went back to his hotel, and early in the morning he was sniffing the streets, his confidence partially returned.

But Emily Price was firmly indoors, or in-tent, as it were, for she had returned to Mrs Jumble's. Sitting in that Worthing cave almost a week ago, shivering, and trying to dismiss the sea's ham-fisted symbolism, she had decided that she wanted to live. In what guise, and where, was secondary and preferable to dying from cold and exposure on the English coastline. So she had taken the last bus back to Brighton and offered some excuse to Mrs Jumble for being so very late. But time meant nothing to Mrs Jumble and she had welcomed her. The week had passed smoothly. Emily enjoyed the simple cooking, and tending to the in-tent plants. Privacy was available whenever she wanted, and sometimes, when Mrs Jumble was asleep, she would wear George Verrey Smith for a while. It was always a relief after her woman-day to feel the rough tweed on her skin, and the solid safety of her lace-up shoes. She wondered whether Mrs Jumble was cheating too in her blue chiffon nightie underneath the donkey blankets. They were both, after all, entitled to their fumbling uncertainties. Sometimes Emily was depressed, especially at night, and then, in her tweeds, she counted her blessings of three meals a day and a roof over her head. Mrs Jumble always did the shopping, so she was safe, but eventually, when she received her wages, she would have to go out and buy another dress. She felt she was beginning to smell and she dreaded each morning on waking that, during the course of the day, Mrs Jumble might refer to it. And the following day, while the Superintendent was prowling Brighton for Emily Price, and the senior officer was scouring London for Washington Jones, and Clive Wentworth, in Stamford Hill, was divining George Verrey Smith, Mrs Jumble noted Emily's sparse wardrobe and offered some clothes of her own until Emily's mythical boxes arrived from London. 'We're practically the same size,' she said. 'You can try them on after supper.'

They were sitting in the tent round a makeshift table, their plates on their knees. Mrs Jumble had put the television on for the news, and it spouted a warming-up hum. Emily worried less about the television. The news of her disappearance was stale, and obviously they had uncovered nothing more. Yet whenever the set was turned on, she tried to mask it or drown it in conversation. But as Mrs Jumble could neither read nor write, it was unfair to cut her off from one of her only means of communication.

'I like to know what's going on in the world,' she would say, turning the switch prior to every news bulletin. She had shown no special interest in the disappearance of George Verrey Smith when it had been announced at the beginning of the week. Even a picture of the man had elicited no comment, though Emily had watched her for the slightest reaction. For herself, she had to grip the arm of her chair. When it appeared on a second bulletin, Emily even ventured to comment on the man's very ordinary appearance. Her vanity prompted her. She could not let her face fill the television frame and remain wholly unnoticed. Mrs Jumble had said that she was quite right. There were a million people who looked like that one, and they'd never find him, an observation that Emily found both a relief and an insult. A later bulletin had suggested Brighton as the man's whereabouts and Mrs Jumble had shown only slightly more interest, to the effect that they should both be careful when they went out. Emily had decided in any case, to lie low until her disappearance had blown over, and now with the promise of Mrs Jumble's clothes, there was even less reason for her to risk the streets. She began to look forward to trying them on, and hoped fervently that Mrs Jumble would leave her alone as she did so. She would have to pretend to be shy and change alone, and then model each garment in front of her. She trembled in anticipation of this new pursuit. Emily Price as a model. She flushed with excitement. She went on eating her salad, though now more daintily. The person of Emily had come much closer to her in the last few days, as the risk of Verrey Smith had worn away. She took more care with her manners and her voice, for being Emily was once more, as in the beginning, enjoyable. She sliced a tomato thinly, and held it daintily on her fork. And as she raised it to her mouth, she heard a familiar voice. It did not belong to Mrs Jumble. She looked at her and that good lady was stuffing her lettuce into her mouth with her hands. She listened intently, and though she could not immediately pinpoint the voice, she felt Emily turning sour inside her once again, and all the joyful anticipation of her after-dinner modelling evaporated. Then she knew the voice as Joy's, but the shock of recognition was too sickening for her to assimilate at the same time the matter of her words. So she had to look squarely at the screen to understand it at all, to see her wife in synchronization before it could mean anything to her. And there Joy was, filling the screen in her indispensable little black, in prepared mourning as it were, talking right at her, begging her to come home. Emily's first reaction was to spit fair and square into her wife's face. She looked at Mrs Jumble out of the corner of her eye, and that lady had stopped lettuce-stuffing and was staring at Joy Verrey Smith. 'Poor woman,' she said, taking advantage of one of the very few pauses that Joy allowed herself in her plea. 'She must be suffering, poor thing.'

'Yes, she is indeed,' Emily agreed, and suddenly felt so too. She could hardly bear to look at her wife's face and its puckered pain. So she listened to what she was saying and tried not to believe that it was she to whom she spoke.

'Dear George,' Joy was saying. 'I don't believe that you have done anything wrong, but I beg you to come home to prove to everybody that you are innocent.' The camera held on her pleading face for some while, and it was clear that she was close to tears.

'Poor woman,' Mrs Jumble said again. 'Pity for her she wants him back. Men don't run away for nothing.'

Emily opened her mouth to deny it, but instead she muttered, 'Poor woman,' as an echo to Mrs Jumble and for a moment she decided that she must go home. It was an irrevocable decision when it was taken, but it lasted for the span of its consideration. She looked at Joy's face and felt for it a disturbing love. She was glad when the camera started to pull back, but what it revealed was even more disturbing. That old eyesore of her childhood, that once-weeping victim, and now the eternal sucker of God-drops. There she sat in her stupid old hat, on Emily's uncut moquette, salivating homilies. It took a while for Emily to take in what she was saying. She hadn't seen her mother for ten years, and there was a certain curiosity in seeing her now, and noticing how little she had changed. She was a weakling still, a victim still, the whipping-boy. All she had done over the years was to swop whippers. Now, after Emily's father, it was the church, and that made whipping almost respectable. She watched her mouth her words without listening to her matter, and she knew by the polite shape of her lips and nostrils that, whatever sermon she was preaching, it was assuredly elocution. Emily looked at Mrs Jumble. 'Poor woman,' she was saying again in the pauses, and Emily thought she was highly indiscriminate.

'It's none of her business,' Emily couldn't help saying.

'But she's his mother,' Mrs Jumble said, and returned to her lettuce-stuffing.

'Go to a church, my son,' his wretched mother was saying with her hat. 'And whatever you have done, confess it. The Lord will give you comfort. Ask His forgiveness, George. His mercy is infinite.'

'Piss off,' Emily said under her breath. Her mother's speech was a death-cell send-off. There was no question in that woman's mind that her son was a compulsive murderer. 'Confess, confess,' she droned on, as she had over the years in her weekly purple.

'Poor woman,' Mrs Jumble said again, still lettuce-stuffing, but with her eye firmly on the box. 'He's probably done away with himself by now anyway. You can see she's praying for his soul.'

And well she might, Emily thought, because George Verrey Smith can be no more.

The camera pulled out once again, to show them both together, the two bereaved women with absolutely nothing in common but their loss. And then they dissolved into a picture of herself, the same passport photograph that they had circulated earlier on in the week. Emily drank her tea, trying to shade her face with her mug. She thought she felt Mrs Jumble looking at her, so she risked putting her tea down. She had to declare that she was hiding nothing. But it was a bad moment; Mrs Jumble's staring, and the voice of the terrible refrain from the box to get in touch with your nearest police-station.

'He's probably left the country,' Emily said, because she simply had to say something.

Mrs Jumble poured more tea, but Emily still felt her stare. Mrs Jumble's lack of reaction to the Verrey Smith disappearance, her near indifference to the whole story, even though he had been reported in Brighton, troubled Emily deeply. She could better have coped with Mrs Jumble's curiosity, some prognosis of the case. But her silence was a possible indication of suspicion, and Emily wondered whether the time had come for her to leave. But the promise of trying on Mrs Jumble's dresses was strong enough to detain her and Mrs Jumble in fact suggested there and then to sort out the clothes. So they went upstairs the two of them, and Emily waited in her room. She wanted to make a show of starting to undress in preparation for the try-on, but she realized that there was really not one article of clothing that she could safely take off, except perhaps the shoes. So she decided to wait until Mrs Jumble came in and then make a show of taking them off. She opened her door so that Mrs Jumble would have no suspicions. Emily was increasingly uneasy. For a moment she thought that Mrs Jumble might be telephoning the police and in a panic she rushed from her room. In the corridor she met a walking mountain of dresses, with Mrs Jumble's little feet propelling them along, and Emily's relief was so great that she hugged her companion through the bundle, and Mrs Jumble, had she had any suspicions hitherto, would certainly have had them dispersed by that gesture.

Together they entered Emily's room. Mrs Jumble laid the clothes on the bed, and Emily sat down and discreetly loosened one shoe. Mrs Jumble watched her and made no move to leave. Emily started on the second shoe, and when that was off, and Mrs Jumble still stood there, she stood up to examine the clothes.

173

'Try them on,' Mrs Jumble said. 'See if they fit.' She stood there still, her arms folded, waiting.

'I know,' said Emily, suddenly inspired, 'you wait in your bedroom, and I'll come inside and model them. I've always wanted to be a model,' she giggled.

'Don't you want any help in zipping them?' Mrs Jumble asked.

'No, let me surprise you,' Emily said, trying with her giggling to reduce it all to a game, so that Mrs Jumble would have shown herself to be a spoil-sport if she did not agree.

'All right,' she said, turning to go. 'I'll go downstairs and turn off the television.'

The telephone was downstairs, and Emily panicked again. She had to dress quickly to interrrupt any investigation Mrs Jumble would pursue. She was more and more disturbed, and the prospect of staying on at Mrs Jumble's, despite the clothes, and the meals and the roof over her head, was less and less favourable. She picked out a red dress from the pile. It was chiffon, and in spite of her growing fears, she could still be stirred by the caress of the material. It was a flowing dress, and it took her some time to outline the neck and to lay it on the bed ready for trying on. Then she took off her clothes, leaving only her underwear, transparently revealing what was left of George Verrey Smith. She threw the dress over her head, shutting her eyes. It was a habit she'd acquired since Emily had overtaken her, the need to see nothing until fully revealed in the mirror. Screwing her eyes tight, she fumbled for the neck opening and slipped it over her head. Then the sleeve openings, and finally she pulled the dress down, shaping it over her body. Then she opened her eyes.

There in the doorway stood Mrs Jumble, smiling. Emily had not heard her come in. If it was only in the last two or three seconds, when her transparency had been covered, then she was in the clear. But how was she to know that she had not arrived while she, Emily, was blindly fumbling with the neckline, while below the bulges, where they should not have been, and the planes where they should, proclaimed a certain freak of nature. And what was Mrs Jumble smiling about? Was it a

174

smile of discovery, a playing along, or was it simply a smile of affection? Emily would never be sure, but she knew it was now too much of a risk to stay to find out.

'That's very pretty,' Mrs Jumble was saying. 'Red's your colour. I prefer it to your black, if you don't mind my saying so. Keep it on. It looks lovely. I'll go down and clear the table. Then let's have a game or two of rummy.'

She was quickly out of the door, and again Emily feared the telephone. It was obvious that she could not go on at such risk. She tore the dress off and replaced it with her well worn black. Even in that she felt safer. She closed her case down, took off her shoes and crept down the stairs. The clatter of the dishes in the kitchen, and the television, which in the end Mrs Jumble hadn't switched off, masked her leaving. She shut the front door behind her, put on her shoes and crept out of the gate. She looked back and gave a silent farewell to Mrs Jumble. If she hadn't cottoned on, then indeed Emily was doing her an act of great discourtesy. If she had, then she was asking for it. Either way, for what she had already done for her, she merited her thanks and farewell.

It was dark outside, and the sound of the sea offensive. Nevertheless, she moved towards it. It was safer than the lamp-lit streets. She crossed over the promenade and down on to the beach. There were a few rocks and the tide was low. Dragging her suitcase, she climbed. She didn't know what to do, and she felt it didn't matter any more. She had come to the end of her own resources. Something was bound to happen, good or bad, to change things. All she knew was that she was past partici-pating in any change. She was weary and depressed, and what strength she had left was channelled into fear. So the sea would do for all that, and this time, she almost welcomed it.

She reached a flat part of the rock, high above the sea, and she sat down, her case between her knees. The sea was calm, and she wondered why, on leaving Mrs Jumble's house, she had heard it roar. She thought perhaps she was hearing only an echo of all the sounds within her, and that, as she had walked to the beach, her waning hopes and gradual abdication had anaesthetized her. She sat there numb, feeling nothing.

Even her fear had drained. She was neither Emily Price, nor George Verrey Smith. She was nothing.

Over on the promenade, the Superintendent, with his not so trusted lieutenant, was taking the night air. All day, the Superintendent had cruised around in a car looking for clues to the whereabouts of Emily Price. Now he needed to stretch himself and, in a brisk walk, to shed the depression that had accumulated during his fruitless day. They stopped and leaned over the railings of the promenade. They were silent, partly because the sight of the sea is a silence-inducing business, but mainly because they had little to say to each other.

The Superintendent scanned the tide-line on the shingle. 'We aren't getting anywhere,' he said, almost to himself.

The lieutenant said nothing. There was nothing he could say to deny it.

'Well,' the Superintendent took his hands off the rails. 'Perhaps something will turn up tomorrow,' he said.

As he raised his eyes from the shingle, he saw the rock and the shape on top of it. 'Coverley,' he said. 'Is that a person out there, or is it a rock shadow?'

'I can't make it out,' Coverley said, following the Superintendent's pointed finger. 'Shall I investigate?'

'I'll come with you,' the Superintendent said. He smelt a find. If it was a person, then that was a find in itself, at this time of night, a person alone on a rock. Not normal. And it just might not be any person. He scrambled down on to the beach, and Coverley followed him. Slowly they climbed the rocks that stretched into the sea. It was very quiet, and the Superintendent motioned Coverley to take off his shoes as he himself was doing. He was now close enough to know that it was no rock that was sitting there. He had seen it move, and his nostrils flared. His eye, a zoom lens, focussed into his target, slowly, gently and with utter precision. He felt in his pocket for his torch. He would use it only at the last moment. He was within a few feet of the figure, and he waited to give it time to turn around.

Emily had heard their footsteps, but she had reached a plane

176

of total indifference to everything. She was not even afraid any more. She knew that there was someone behind her, but inertia had conquered all curiosity. She sensed a torch light over her shoulder, and then obliquely in her face. She squinted a little, and heard a man's voice.

'Anything wrong, Madam? What are you doing out here?' He couldn't imagine why anyone should make such a journey to sit on a rock jutting out to sea unless there were something radically wrong.

Emily didn't answer. The light caught her face once more.

'What's your name, Madam?'

'Emily Price.' She knew it as an innocent enough name that betrayed nothing.

The Superintendent slipped on the rock. He felt he had walked into a copse where a calm fox sat waiting. He couldn't believe his good fortune, and he wanted to savour it a little to make it last. 'Pardon?' he said.

'Emily Price.' Loud and clear.

'Mrs or Miss?'

'Mrs,' she said. 'I am a widow.'

Better and better. He took out his notebook. 'I've been looking for you,' he said as casually as he could.

And then fear melted her, wondering by what misfortune she had chosen a name that was on the wanted list, and for what crime she was being sought.

'Emily Price,' the Superintendent was saying, and it echoed over the sea, magnifying whatever the crime was she was wanted for. Coverley, who by now had tardily reached his chief, gasped in astonishment. Emily shivered. But she was less frightened now. She knew that George Verrey Smith was wanted for murder. Emily Price could be wanted for no worse. She possibly had a double murder on her head, and if her mother had anything to say in the matter, a triple. And in all that, even the latter, she felt totally innocent. She smiled a little, at the ridiculous complexity of the situation. She had brought it about, it was true, but now it was out of her hands.

'I would like you to accompany us to the station,' the Superintendent said.

'Why?' she asked automatically, though she was only faintly curious about the nature of the charge.

'I would like to question you in connection with the disappearance of George Verrey Smith,' he said.

She got up as if summoned, and picked up her case.

'You need not say anything at the moment,' the Superintendent said gently. He could afford kindness now. Wearing her down would come later. 'Let me carry that for you,' he said. He'd taken it from her hand before she could protest, and with it her incriminating alibi. Coverley helped her over the rocks. They both behaved like gentlemen, and when they reached the promenade, they discreetly hemmed her in on either side. To the odd passer-by they were three middle-aged residents, taking the evening air. One actually acknowledged them. 'Fine night,' he said, in passing, and the Superintendent readily agreed. He had not had a finer night in years.

When they reached the station, they sat her down with her case in front of her. They made no move to open it. It was, as yet, none of their business. They offered her a cup of coffee, and the Superintendent sent Coverley away. He asked for a clerk to come in and take whatever statement would be forthcoming. Then he sat down opposite her and lit a cigarette. He waited for her to finish her coffee, then he leaned forward, smiling. 'Mrs Price,' he said. 'I want you to tell me everything. George Verrey Smith is wanted by the police in connection with the murder of Samuel Parsons in London a week ago. We know that he is in Brighton, and that you have been with him. It is in your interest to tell us everything you know. You yourself are not a suspect, unless of course you continue to harbour one. I want you to tell me everything for your own sake.' He leaned back, satisfied that it was a good beginning.

She said nothing, but he was prepared to wait. Waiting was part of the game. It was a basic rule in police investigation. You were more likely to get the truth after a period of contemplation, than in an immediate gush of compulsive confession. So he waited, twiddling his thumbs, and looking at her.

'I don't know,' she said at last. 'I've never heard of Mr Smith. I read about it in the papers, that's all.'

'You telephoned his wife about a week ago.' The Superintendent came to the point. 'You told her he was with you. I
have a tape of your conversation.'

'Emily Price is a common enough name,' she rallied. 'It
could have been another one.'

'You have a distinctive voice, Mrs Price,' the Superintendent
said. 'It checks admirably with my recording.'

'I don't know anything about it,' she said.

Well, he could wait. This woman was his quarry. Of that
there was no question. He could afford to play with it for a
while. 'Where do you live, Mrs Price?' he asked.

She gave him Mrs Jumble's address because she had to say
something. 'And do you work?' he said.

'I am Mrs Jumble's housekeeper-companion.'

'Have you lived in Brighton long?'

'No,' she said, and gave him the same story she had given to
Mrs Jumble, moving him, she hoped, with her widowhood and
her reduced circumstances.

The Superintendent was sympathetic. 'It's hard for a woman
alone,' he said gently. 'D'you mind opening your case?'

She started. She had not considered that eventuality, and
had no idea of how to explain its contents. But it was now all
beyond her. She knew she could come out bluntly with the
whole truth, and perhaps she should, she thought, for her own
and desperate good. But in her indecision, as always, Emily
clung to her. Emily didn't want to die. She had found a home
in her, and her voice insisted in its gentleness. 'Let me be, let
me be,' it told her. 'We're lost without each other.'

Emily opened the case, and as she did so, she said, 'This isn't
my case. I took it by mistake from Mrs Jumble's.'

The Superintendent laughed aloud. It was such a poor lie
coming from an obviously intelligent woman, and he told her
so, in friendly fashion. 'Anyway,' he said, 'even if it's Mrs
Jumble's, let's see what's inside.'

Even the Superintendent, with his supreme optimism, was
not prepared for the rich vein of evidence that the opened
suitcase revealed. He salivated, taking the clothes out one by
one. The check jacket that Mrs Verrey Smith had remembered,

the grey trousers. He held them up in front of him. It was not difficult for him to see George Verrey Smith inside them.

'Well,' he said. 'Well, well.' He'd been patient long enough. He'd waited long enough. He'd been polite for too long. He banged his fist on the table, making it quite clear to the startled Emily that the courtesies were over. 'Where is he?' he thundered. 'What have you done with him?'

'Nothing,' she stammered. 'I don't know him.'

'Mrs Price,' the Superintendent said. 'I don't have to tell you how much you are already implicated in all this. These clothes belong to George Verrey Smith. Their identification is only a formality. They are in your possession. The clothes of a suspect murderer. That doesn't look too good for you, Mrs Price,' he warned. 'Where is he?' he shouted. And then, in almost a whisper, 'Or should I say, where is his body?'

She trembled and opened her mouth with the truth. But Emily stifled her with almost a soprano plea. She shut her mouth obediently. Now was no time to be George Verrey Smith. He was dead, as the Superintendent implied, and probably, in his mind, at the bottom of the sea. He would be there waiting at high tide to identify the washed up body. For him it was only a question of time. But she owed it to Emily to stand by her, to identify herself wholly with what had been hitherto only a name. She had to accept Emily totally. She had to love her. 'My name is Emily Price,' she said, and it was a declaration of absolute faith.

'I'm well aware of that,' the Superintendent said, puzzled by this seeming irrelevancy. 'What I want to know, is the whereabouts of George Verrey Smith.'

'I have nothing to say,' she said.

'Then I'll give you time to think of something.' He turned to the clerk. 'Take this lady to the cells,' he said. 'If you should change your mind, Mrs Price, about talking, you know, please inform me through your guard. I can wait, Mrs Price. I can wait a long time, and I have a feeling I can wait longer than you.'

She got up without protest and made to pick up her case.

'I don't think you'll be needing that,' the Superintendent

said. 'It's a valuable piece of evidence, and it belongs, if I may say so, to the police.'

Emily let herself be led out. She was comforted by her re-conciliation with herself. She must never be anybody else any more. Emily was her refuge and her strength. She was her dignity too. Poor George. She would never think of him again. He would have to find his own death without her.

The Superintendent sat at his desk. This was the best part of a case, when the threads lay there for your assembly. He examined the clothes again. There was nothing in the pockets, and a faint smell of perfume hung about them. He put them back into the case. It was going to be hard on Mrs Verrey Smith, but it was imperative that she identify them. The implications of the uninhabited clothes were terrible. But he would be gentle with her and understanding, as they always were on television. But he had his job to do and, after all, it wasn't such a bad job. Maybe, the film business wasn't such a good idea for his son. There was a greater sense of service in the Police. Yes, he'd suggest it.

And immediately, he thought of Washington Jones. There'd been no news from London. The boy's disappearance was the only factor that marred his full enjoyment of having run Mrs Price to ground. He would get on to headquarters right away. He had to contact Mrs Verrey Smith too, but that would have to wait till the morning. He'd go back to his hotel, and let Mrs Emily Price stew. Serves her right for being so respectable.

10

Joy Verrey Smith and Mrs Whitely waited in the ante-room. Mr Clive Wentworth was a very busy man. His clients came from far and wide, and though it was still early morning, he was already running late. His appointment after Mrs Whitely's had already arrived. She didn't believe in this sort of thing, she told Mrs Whitely, but you had to do something, didn't you. The police were no good. They weren't interested in missing persons unless they'd been kidnapped, or were running away from the Law. Her husband had been gone for three years, and not a word from him. 'It's not that I grieve any more,' she said. 'It's just that I'd like to know where I stand. He's got a nice fat life insurance, but they won't pay up until he's gone without trace for seven years, and I could do with the money, I can tell you.'

She held an old vest in her hand, all that stood between her and the insurance. She was crumpling it in her hand, hating it, and all it stood for. 'You've got to bring something with you, you know, an article of clothing. Have you got something? They need it for the vibrations. I know, because I've been to so many. They all say something different. But this one's supposed to be very good. They come from foreign parts to see him. I'd have brought something else, but this was all he left. He took every stitch of clothing with him.' She was crumpling the vest as she spoke and it probably by now contained more of her vibrations than his, apart from those of the string of diviners through whose hands it had already passed. 'They tell you not to put it in a paper bag,' she said. 'It damps down the pulses.'

The word was obviously not part of the woman's normal running vocabulary. It was part of the jargon she'd picked up diviner-traipsing. The woman's fruitless search had a depressing effect on Joy. 'I told you there was no point in coming,' she said to her mother-in-law.

'He's got a marvellous reputation,' Mrs Whitely said. 'Now take his pants out of the paper bag. This lady,' she smiled at the other client, 'is more experienced in this kind of thing. We can save time if we save the vibrations.'

Joy opened the paper bag and pulled out George's pants. There had been some discussion at home as to what article of clothing they should choose. Joy had thought to herself that one of his sunday dresses would have been a more reliable barometer to George's pulse. It was Mrs Whitely who had suggested that intimate article, because she felt, though she did not say as much, that there would be an overflow of vibrations in that receptacle. It was a mother talking about her son, without any logic but with total intuition. Joy had deferred to her choice, sensing that she herself understood so little about her husband in that area, that her mother-in-law could not have understood less. So they had lovingly wrapped George's pants in brown paper, and according to this woman had probably already robbed them of all pulse. So Joy rubbed them in her hand as the woman was doing, to erase the torpor of the paper wrapping.

'Who have you got missing?' the woman said.

'My son,' Mrs Whitely answered, taking full responsibility.

'Has he been gone long?'

'Just over a week.'

'You're very sensible,' the woman said. 'I waited for over a year before I came to one of these. The tracks get covered if you leave it too long. And my husband was a wily one. Cunning? He could have given a fox lessons.' As far as she was concerned, her lost husband was strictly in the past tense. She didn't want to find him. All she wanted was her widowhood confirmed. She wanted to know the whereabouts of his body, so that she could drag the insurance agent there to look at it and see for himself. 'Show us the body,' they had said, 'and you can collect.' And she was going to find it. He couldn't hide his corpse, cunning though he was.

'Have you given up hope of his being alive?' Joy said. She didn't like the woman. Her attitudes invalidated any hope that she had of ever seeing George again.

'I wish him dead,' the woman said. At least she was being honest. 'I was like you,' she went on, 'hoping and hoping. But in the end, whether he's dead or alive, he's got to be dead for you. You can't go on, hoping and hoping.'

The consulting-room door opened, and a man came out, clutching a silk petticoat. He'd obviously mislaid his wife and by the sombre look on his face, he had received small clue as to her whereabouts. As he closed the door, a bell rang, obviously the signal for the next client. 'Wish you luck,' the woman said as they went inside, and she screwed up the vest in her hand, and idly began to chew it.

Mr Clive Wentworth was wearing a white coat, for he looked upon his profession as a branch of science. He got up from his desk to greet them, carefully stepping over a large map of Asia spread out on the floor. It had obviously met the needs of the last client whose wife had apparently had inclinations to the Far East. Mr Wentworth asked them to be seated while he rolled up his map. Then he himself sat down behind the desk and looked at them. 'Who is the spokesman?' he said.

Joy Verrey Smith and her mother-in-law looked at each other. It was Joy's priority, of course, but she would have happily relinquished it to Mrs Whitely. The latter responded by opening her bag and taking out her rosary. If there were any mumbo-jumbo around, it would be as well to lay one's hands on any old tool to exorcise it.

'I'm his wife,' Joy said, 'the wife of the man who has disappeared, and this is his mother.' She was plainly putting the decision in his hands.

'Then perhaps Mrs – er –'

'Verrey Smith,' she gave him.

'Then perhaps, Mrs Verrey Smith, junior, you had better tell me the whole story. But before you start,' he said, 'could you give me that garment?'

She passed it over the desk, and he laid it out flat on the palm of his hand. 'Now begin,' he said. Mr Wentworth made notes

184

with his other hand. Occasionally he would ask her to stop, while he closed his eyes, trembled and made a note on his pad with a pen containing invisible ink. These pauses threw Joy somewhat, and then Mrs Whitely would cue her. But Mrs Whitely's interruptions threw Mr Wentworth, and he was on the point of asking her to leave, but she begged his pardon with the old timidity that Joy remembered.

Joy was very forthcoming, and Mr Wentworth asked very few questions. She told him everything that was already publicly known, and added the telephone call from Mrs Price in Brighton. She would have told him about Tommy as well, but for the presence of her mother-in-law. The Tommy affair was strictly private, but she would have told Mr Wentworth about it because there was an aura of safe anonymity about him. When she had come to the end of her story, Mr Wentworth asked her if he could hold her hand for a while. Mrs Whitely gasped at the sexual overtones of the request, and frantically counted her beads. Joy held out her hand, and he held it over his head. 'Now tell me again,' he said, 'the name of your husband, his age, his profession and what he was wearing when you saw him last.'

Joy obliged once again. Mr Wentworth's eyes were closed, and as she spoke, he placed George's pants over their locked hands. Joy shivered and he let her hand go. Then he went over to his cupboard and took out a large rolled map. This he unfurled on the floor. It was a map of England in great physical and political detail. Having set it out, he asked them to leave him and to wait in the ante-room. He would call them when he was ready.

And so once again, they joined the insurance-seeker, chewing on her obstacle as if in prelude to total consumption. They sat down opposite her. She stopped chewing. 'Any news?' she asked.

'We have to wait,' Mrs Whitely said.

'What did he do? Did he hold your hand?'

Joy nodded. She didn't particularly want to enter into a conversation. For some reason she had faith in this man, and she didn't want him spoken about by a tepid believer. She felt that he was divinely and therefore temporarily inspired and that, as soon as she was gone, he would forget the name of George Verrey Smith and all his story. She decided to believe in him, whatever he had to offer. But if, on the other hand, he located George's corpse – she shuddered at the thought – then of course, the man was an imposter and a fraud.

'I went to a man once,' the woman was saying. 'Told me my husband was in the south of France. Well I told the police, but they weren't very interested, and I couldn't go down myself to find out. I mean, I didn't want to spend all the insurance money in advance, and in the end not get it because the bast-ard's still alive.' She took to her chewing again.

'A pleasant man,' Mrs Whitely offered, more to her daughter-in-law than to the other woman. She felt it inadvisable to speak badly of the man. He might sense it, and give them news to spite them. 'He seems very serious to me. I, for one, am prepared to go by what he says.'

This declaration seemed to silence them all. The woman opened her holdall, and took out a packet of sandwiches. She was used to this kind of thing. Waiting in waiting-rooms, if not for people-diviners, then for fortune-tellers and the like. And in fact, she volunteered some information of the latter after her snack, and before the resumption of her chewing. 'I went to a fortune-teller once,' she said. 'Told me I'd be married again within the year. That was two years ago. How can I get married again,' she asked no one in particular, 'if I don't know whether or not I'm a widow?'

'I'm sure it'll all come out all right,' Joy said. She was get-ting very restless, anxious for the man's verdict, and the wo-man's constant chatter got on her nerves. She got up and paced the room, counting her steps, giving herself fifty before knocking at his door, and then, at forty-nine, another fifty, to give the man a chance. On the second round, they heard his bell, but neither made a move towards the door. Suddenly Joy didn't want to know any more, and Mrs Whitely too, was loath to hear his verdict. The bell rang once more.

'I know what it feels like,' the woman said, 'but you never know, he's probably a fraud like the rest of them.'

As she gave her verdict, Mr Wentworth opened the door himself to find out the reason for the delay.

'She said that,' Mrs Whitely said quickly, pointing to the woman, anxious to exonerate herself and her daughter-in-law from such a blasphemous opinion.

Mr Wentworth stared at the woman, who, sensing that she had already lost her own private battle, stuffed her husband's vest back into her holdall, and made for the door.

'What you have said, Madam,' Mr Wentworth called after her, 'cannot in any way influence my findings in your case. Please stay. I'm sure I can help you.'

The woman turned and sulked back into her chair. Then she took out the vest again, and shook it out to bring it back to consciousness. 'I'm ready for you now,' Mr Wentworth was saying, and he held the door open for the two ladies.

The map had been taken away, and George's pants lay life-less on the desk. He took a paper bag from his drawer and put the pants inside. He handed them over. It was a terrible omen. He'd come to his own conclusion and he himself was killing the vibrations because, as far as he was concerned, a second opinion was totally unnecessary. 'A very interesting case,' he began. 'I've never had one quite like it.'

Joy fidgeted. She was not interested in the history of his case diagnoses. She just wanted to know about her George. 'D'you know where he is?' she said. 'Is he alive?' She regretted having asked it. That called for only a Yes or No answer. It was altogether too final. 'D'you know where he is?' she said again, hoping that its repetition would erase the question she had regretted.

'I have bad news for you,' he said, though there was no sympathy in his voice, and the very lack of it, for some reason, confirmed the faith that Joy had in him. She was going to have to believe him, she knew. This man had no axe to grind. He was guided by a simple faith, and he abided by whatever truth that faith revealed.

'George Verrey Smith,' he said, 'is dead. Of that, there is no doubt.'

Mrs Whitely took her daughter-in-law's hand. 'Don't believe

it,' she said. 'It's all mumbo-jumbo. You're the work of the devil,' she shouted at Mr Wentworth. 'If my son is dead, then where is his body? Why hasn't that been found?'

'That's what's so very interesting about the case,' Mr Wentworth went on, unperturbed. 'Although George Verrey Smith is dead, and of that there is no question, he does not seem to have left a corpse behind.'

'Then he must have risen,' Mrs Whitely scoffed. Then suddenly hearing her blasphemy, she hastily crossed herself, and took to counting her beads again. 'Let's go, Joy,' she said, getting up. 'I must go to confession. This was all a terrible sin.'

But Joy did not move. 'Why are you so sure he's dead?' Joy said. 'And where did he die?'

'I cannot explain certain things to you,' he said. 'There exist no words to explain certain phenomena. I know he is dead,' he said, 'because the pulse is gone from his clothing. I think that he died here in London, although there is the sea all about him. Yet his body is neither on land nor the water. Neither,' he added, in case she was going to suggest it, 'has it been consumed by the fire. I have no guidance whatsoever as to where it is. I simply know with absolute certainty, that George Verrey Smith is no more.' He put his hand on her arm. 'I'm very sorry,' he said, and Joy sensed that he meant it, but for some reason, it was out of character. She was putting the pants in her bag. There was nothing she could say, except that she believed him. Her mother-in-law was already at the door. She followed her out silently. The woman in the waiting-room let up on her chewing, and seeing Joy's crestfallen face, she said, 'He's only right if you believe in him,' and as she left the room, Joy felt that the people-diviner was not Mr Wentworth, but the woman waiting outside for her widowhood.

'Don't fret yourself,' Mrs Whitely kept saying on the way home, but Joy knew that she too was worried. There was still the phone call from the little boy, that fading ray of hope, but Joy knew that that only cleared George of murder. It was no guarantee that he was still alive. She started to cry, already to mourn him. 'We mustn't believe that man,' Mrs Whitely said with very little self-confidence. 'Come with me to the church,' she said. 'We'll wait for confession. We've done a sinful thing by putting our faith in false prophets. Confession will do you good, my dear. It's an ill wind,' she muttered.

'I'm going home,' Joy said. 'George may be ringing. I've got to be there for him.'

'Yes,' Mrs Whitely said. 'Perhaps that's better for you at the moment. Hold on to your faith. I shall come back later. The Lord will give us guidance. We are punished for our folly.'

They parted at the corner and Joy went home. As she turned into her street, she could see a police car parked in front of her door, and a number of net curtains were raised. She panicked, knowing that there was news of George. She ran towards her house and, as she reached the gate, a policeman got out of the car. He was of high rank by his uniform, and he took her arm as they walked up the drive. Now she knew from his courtesy that the news was bad.

'Shall we go inside, Mrs Verrey Smith?' he asked.

Joy opened the door and they went into the kitchen. Spit and Polish welcomed them with inappropriate twirpings. She sat down because she knew that what the policeman had to say was going to shake her.

'I have to ask you, Mrs Verrey Smith,' he said, 'to come with me to Brighton. A suitcase of clothes has been found. We think they may belong to your husband. We need you to identify them.'

'Oh, my God,' she whispered. 'Then he really is dead.' She shook with her sobbing, and the policeman put his hand on her shoulder.

'It doesn't mean that necessarily,' he said. 'Nothing like that has been proved. Would you like to make yourself a cup of tea first?' he said, 'and then I can drive you down.'

She didn't feel like tea or any kind of delay. She wanted to go to Brighton quickly and identify possibly all that was left of George. The continued unknowing was terrible. But she had, out of courtesy, to wait until her mother-in-law came back, yet she did not want her with her in Brighton. She didn't want to tell her about the suitcase, but how could she explain her necessary departure. She was angry that her mother-in-law had come at all, whose presence necessitated such devious excuses. She had enough grief without the need to conceal it. Somehow it wasn't fair. So she went next door to Mrs Johnson and gave her the key, asking her to look out for her mother-in-law. She herself was going to see one of George's school colleagues. That would have to be good enough. Then she left the house quickly, the policeman following her.

They exchanged not a word during the whole journey to Brighton. Joy sobbed most of the way and, when they reached the station, it was some time before she could bring herself to get out of the car.

11

Inside, in a square cell, Emily waited, battling with Emily. The more dangerous the liaison, the greater her reluctance to give it up. Emily sang like a swan inside her. She was in trouble. She knew that. Her possession of George's clothes pointed at her as his murderer. Yet she had wanted to kill George, as she had wanted to kill her father, but the fact that she had wanted both of them dead, had nothing to do with murder. Emily had told her in no uncertain terms that, if she went back to George, her father was part of that package too.

She heard footsteps in the corridor. They were coming for her. She took her powder compact from her bag, and renewed her make-up. Emily smiled at her through the mirror, a faint smile of blackmail. She put her compact away as a policeman opened the cell door.

'Follow me,' he said, and she went after him, her Emily steps dragging her, so that he had to wait. He took her back to the reception where she had first been taken, and he knocked on the door. Then he threw the door open wide, and allowed Emily to pass through. She saw her wife standing there in front of the open suitcase, and weeping, and she knew she must stifle any sign of recognition.

The Superintendent did not ask her to sit down. Courtesy was no longer in order. Emily felt Joy staring at her. Through her tears there was a squint of terrible recognition. 'I know her,' Joy blurted out. 'I've seen her before. She was at Mr Johnson's funeral.'

The Superintendent put his hand on her arm.

'Where's my husband?' she screamed at Emily. 'Where is he?'

The policeman on the other side tried to calm her, to sit her down, to take from her hand a piece of George's clothing that she clasped to her breast. Then she sat on the chair and broke down completely, sobbing uncontrollably into her husband's shirt.

'Mrs Emily Price,' the Superintendent said with great ceremony. 'I am arresting you on a charge of suspicion of murder of George Verrey Smith.'

Emily trembled, but there was no fear in her. She wallowed in the positive orgasm of her deception. No. She would not leave Emily. There was too much joy through her, too much truth to be denied. But Joy's anguish tore through her. She had to hold on to herself to prevent herself from moving forward to comfort her.

'George,' Joy was whimpering. 'My beloved George.' She looked hard at Emily. 'He was a good man,' she sobbed. 'He wouldn't have hurt anybody. You've taken away my life.'

That was the turning point for Emily. It screamed at her for a decision. Well, she thought, there was always the study and the sunday dressing. There was teaching, an income, a home. There was Mrs Johnson, and oh my God, there was Tommy. It was not much of a choice, but Joy's heartbreaking sobbing made it for her. Gentle, gentle Emily. She would never forgive her. She had to say something. They were all staring at her, wondering why she showed no fear. Well, she would try. She knew it was a question of her life. But her heart was not in it.

'I am George Verrey Smith,' she tried. She was moved by the Emily voice that insisted out of her. It was pleading and gentle. Emily didn't want to die, and George was loath to bury her.

'I am George Verrey Smith,' she tried again, and this time the old thrill of that non-hyphened name vibrated just a little. She tried again, as if turning a string, plucking it occasionally for its true pitch. And as it settled, her voice lost its plea, and took on the old and known resonance. She yielded for the last time. 'I am George Verrey Smith,' she croaked. Poor Emily.

'And I'm George Washington,' the Superintendent said. And that reminded him with sudden fear. Had Washington Jones been found? He must go back to London. 'Come along, Mrs Price,' he said, fastening the suitcase.

'I am George Verrey Smith,' she insisted, and knew from their hostile response that she had to make a final gesture. She raised her hand to her head and hesitated. Then slowly she lifted the wig, and placed it tenderly on the table. Joy looked at her, and managed to whisper, 'George.' She attempted to come towards him but, on rising from her chair, she swayed and fell on the Superintendent's arm. He passed her gently on to the policeman for revival.

The Superintendent picked up the wig from the table and screwed it up in his hand with rage. George thought he heard Emily cry.

'Well, Mr Verrey Smith,' the Superintendent said, regaining his calm. 'In that case, it's only a question of rephrasing the charge. George Verrey Smith. I arrest you on suspicion of the murder of Samuel Parsons.'

George was silent. He had no choice now but to give Emily a decent burial and, as he folded her into his heart, his father roared out of his grave like a lion.

Part Three

12

I have not been very well. I've been out of countenance and circulation for some while, and I think that this confession has had a lot to do with it. But things are easier now, and the urge to write comes upon me once again. But I wonder to myself why it should be like that, that we attempt to cure ourselves of something, and the attempt itself confounds us. I started out in good faith to tell you everything, and then confession laid me low. It's a lesson, I suppose, to keep one's mouth shut, and to get on with one's living, in private. But once a confession is started, a mistake in itself, it is a greater mistake to leave it half-told.

I was telling you about my father, and then a series of events overtook me and silenced me for a while. They are not important, and have nothing to do with my confession, but out of courtesy I shall relate them briefly, for they do account for the hiatus in this narrative.

You may remember that there was trouble with Mr Parsons at the school. You may remember also that I defended him. I knew then I would have to pay for it, and indeed I did, for the poor devil was found murdered a few days later, and I, for a variety of reasons which I don't want to go into now, I, George Verrey Smith, was suspect number one.

Mr Parsons had met a particularly horrible death behind the maintenance shed, a location which was apparently his second home. He had just besported himself with Washington Jones, one of our coloured quota from the lower third, and the latter, five bob the richer, was just leaving the shed when he heard Parsons talking to a man, and both voices were raised. Washington, being a healthy curious lad, peeped round the wall of the shed, and overheard and saw what took place. And thank

God for Washington, or I would now be languishing in a cell awaiting punishment, instead of getting all this off my chest, though I know from experience that it will not make me feel any better. Anyway, it was Washington's evidence that saved my neck, and out of respect for him, I give it to you in his own words.

'Me and Mister Parsons was doing 'omework, m'lud, be'ind the shed. Then when we was finished, I went round the corner, an' I 'eard Mister Chipple – that's 'im over there in the box – an' 'e was shouting at Mister Parsons, an' 'e was 'olding a knife. They was talking very loud, an' 'im over there, 'e said that the money were due, an' 'e 'adn't been paid for two months, and 'e'd 'ad 'is last chance. An' Mister Parsons, 'e said 'e wasn't gonna pay no more, never, 'e said, 'cos 'e'd been found out anyway, and 'e could say wot 'e liked to anybody, 'e wasn't gettin' another penny. Then I saw Mister Chipple put the knife in 'is stomach an' in 'is back. An' then Mister Parsons fell down an' Mister Chipple undone Mister Parsons's trouser, an' then – well, you know wot 'e done. Then I screamed. I couldn't 'elp it, an' Mister Chipple saw me, an' I ran, an' 'e came after me, but 'e couldn't catch me 'cos 'e's too fat. And then one day after school, 'e was waiting, an' I didn't see 'im, an' 'e got me an' 'e took me in a car. We was in the country somewhere, an' when we got out, I ran away, an' 'e followed an' 'e fell down. That's why e's got 'is leg in plaster. No, m'lud. We was only doin' 'omework. Mister Parsons always 'elped some of the boys after school.'

Washington was a great one for the euphemism. He probably learned more about life behind that maintenance shed than through Mr Parsons's orthodox teaching practices. For though it is not done to speak ill of the dead, between you and me, Mr Parsons was a rotten teacher. He told me himself he only did it for the connections. Now I understand what he meant. Poor devil.

Of course, while I was under suspicion, the Cloth thought it advisable for me to absent myself from the school until the whole business was cleared up. Which I did. It took a few weeks in all, and I was out of countenance most of the time.

When it was all over, insofar as this sort of business can ever be over – once cited, suspicion lingers, no matter how innocent the accused – the Cloth called on me to resume my duties. I was hesitant. Something had happened during my indisposition that prompted a certainty in me that things could not go on as before. A radical change had to come about, and a change of job and even location would perhaps be a beginning. So I hesitated. The Cloth begged me to return.

A likely story, you are probably thinking. Hardly possible, you would assume, that after all my philanderings, the Cloth would want me back. He might ask, certainly, as a mere formality, hoping to God I would refuse of my own accord. But beg? Out of the question. Well, you can believe what you like. This is my confession and I can do what I like with it. He begged. Believe it or not, he begged.

I rather liked that, the Cloth begging. Even Miss Price, who in my absence had come to value my services, urged me, on her own behalf, to return to their merry band. There they both were, practically on their knees. I let them go on for a bit, but not too long, because in supplication, unless absolutely certain of one's cause, there comes a moment of gross humiliation, and the cause itself is then in rage, discounted. I saw Miss Price's lower lip tremble, and I took that as a sign to assert the rightness of their plea. 'I am honoured that you should value me so highly,' I said, and they trembled, hope bursting their seams.

'Then you will return?' the Cloth said meekly.

I smiled at him.

'I knew you would,' he said. He actually put his hand on my arm. I let it lie there for a while, smiling still. Then I took it up with the tips of my fingers, and dropped it off, like an earwig.

'You know where you can stick your lousy job,' I said. 'And fuck you, too, Miss Price,' I added. 'You should be so lucky.'

I walked out of the Cloth's study. After the manner of my departure, I couldn't hope for a reference from him, and I knew better than to ask. I had won the game as long as I was prepared not to prolong it. So I left in the ascendant, albeit without testimonial, but every second of that interview had been worthwhile.

Now I know you're possibly thinking that I have tailored this whole story to suit my own vanity. Well, you may take my word for it. It was I who gave the Cloth the boot. For what other reason would he have refused me a reference? And moreover, it didn't turn out to be such a handicap. I have since learned, that dotted all over the English countryside, skulking behind the stained glass of erstwhile stately homes, there lies many a teaching establishment, where a testimonial from an orthodox school is positively an impediment. They are run, in the main, by unfrocked headmasters and staffs with histories similar to my own. Many of them look uncommonly like the late Mr Parsons. All have, in their time, taught within the confines of the establishment, but all have felt that establishment as a prison, and an obstacle to imaginative teaching. So they group together to pursue a rather less orthodox teaching method, and in my new school, you can take my word for it, there is much of that. But I am content enough here. My wife, too, has taken happily to the countryside, and there are enough good works to occupy her, including, I may add, the collection of signatures of those who wish to close down my school. Sometimes I give a thought to poor Chipple and the bars that he must contemplate for a quarter of a century. Sometimes I think of Tommy but with little affection. He told my wife everything when I was out of countenance, but I've cleared all that up now. I rarely give a thought to Mrs Johnson, and if I do, it is with pity. I have cleared out my mind considerably since my indisposition. I have gone into the corners and the crevices, and fumigated all. I have come to know myself a little, not in any positive sense, perhaps. But there is also some wisdom in knowing what one is not. For a moment, during my confession to you, I thought I had traced some outline of identity. I recall a distinct euphoria at the time. But in the end, it was too frail to sustain itself. Now, in my own unsure frame of George Verrey Smith, age, er, forty-two, by profession a schoolmaster, with no longer any confidence in my teeth, I know, and this my confession has taught me – I know that I am neither man nor woman. I say it aloud. I am neither man nor woman, and the absence of an echo, confirms its truth. I write it down. I am neither man nor woman, and it is but the signature to the declaration of my own limbo. That is all.

Then what am I? Yes, I have cleared out my mind, but I must confess, after all this confession, that there still remains a millstone, central, whole, solid and immovable. My father lodges in my skull, a stubborn sitting-tenant. I have confessed to his murder. I have made excuses, I have lied, but in the end, and between the lines, you have prised out my ignominy. I am a murderer. I stand before you like a time-honoured alcoholic seeking the cure. I confess it publicly, that which I really am.

Shall I tell the priest? He will tell me perhaps to go to the Police. And I will go to the station and say, 'Excuse me, Officer, but just over thirty years ago, I killed my father.' And he, reckoning my years, will humour me. So I have chosen to confess it to you, you, whom I do not know, and cannot envisage, and from you, there is no come-back. That is the hardest confession of all. It is the kind of confession that is not good for the soul. From such confession there is no pay-off, no orgasm of punishment. Yet punishment is essential for what I have learned myself to be. And since there is no one to administer it, I must organize my own retribution.

I have put away my sundays. The pain of such a loss is punishment enough, believe me. But I have had to do it, for my sundays were an escape route, and I must face what I am, for ever, and without let-up. I have given them all away, even my wig, for they interfered with my obsession, with my blemish, with my stain. I am a murderer. My father stiffens in my skull, like a corpse awaiting post-mortem, and I cannot bury him until the coroner is satisfied. He died, I know, because I wished him dead. The trip wire was only incidental. It was my studied and persistent will that killed him, and in what part of his body could be found proof of that, and in any case, what coroner in the land would sanction it? So he lies stinking out of my head, and I know that in the end, he will outlive me. His fulsome stench will flush me out of my own frame.

201

Sometimes I am sorry that I gave away my sundays. I would have liked to look at them, just to look, from time to time. Perhaps one day, when Joy is out, I'll have a tiny try-on, just a little one. Of course, I wouldn't go out in them, ever ever again. Unless of course it was very dark, and I could cross the fields unseen. Even as I think about it, and write it down, my thoughts are creeping towards her wardrobe.

But why should I tell you all this? I have told you enough, more than you ever needed to know, and certainly more than was good for me. I'm leaving you now, which is the only way I can get rid of you. I am going. That was true what I said about my sundays. I promise you they're over and done with. Not even a little look. Not even a tiny try-on. Not even a . . .

I'm going now. I've got to. Don't try and stop me. There are things I have to do.